W9-AAL-416

DEATH

& the Redheaded Woman

LORETTA ROSS

DEATH

& the Redheaded Woman

An
Auction Block
MYSTERY

MIDNIGHT INK
WOODBURY, MINNESOTA

Death and the Redheaded Woman © 2015 by Loretta Ross. All rights reserved. No part of this book may be used or reproduced in any manner whatsoever, including Internet usage, without written permission from Midnight Ink, except in the case of brief quotations embodied in critical articles and reviews.

Book design and format by Donna Burch-Brown
Cover design by Lisa Novak
Cover illustration: © Tim Zeltner/www.i2iart.com; additional images: iStock-
   photo.com/993745/© NNehring; shutterstock/96002282/©Repina Valeriya
Editing by Connie Hill

Midnight Ink, an imprint of Llewellyn Worldwide Ltd.

This is a work of fiction. Names, characters, places, and incidents are either the product of the author's imagination or are used fictitiously, and any resemblance to actual persons, living or dead, business establishments, events, or locales is

ISBN 978-1-62953-430-5

Midnight Ink
Llewellyn Worldwide Ltd.
2143 Wooddale Drive
Woodbury, MN 55125-2989

Printed in the United States of America

This book is dedicated, with love, to the memory of my parents:

EDWARD LAMONT ROSS

and

EMMA ALICE (EMERSON) ROSS

ACKNOWLEDGMENTS

Becoming a published author is a lifelong dream for me, but it is one that I never could have accomplished on my own. I'd like to take this opportunity to thank the following people for their help and kindness.

First and foremost, I'd like to thank my family for overlooking my many and varied eccentricities and never, even once, trying to have me committed. I'd also like to thank them for unwittingly providing me with unlimited material, even if my agent makes me cut most of it because it's "too bizarre to be believed."

I'd like to thank all the wonderful people online who read and commented on my early attempts at writing. Their encouragement was invaluable and I learned more from their constructive feedback than I ever could have from books or writing courses. I'd particularly like to thank the members of the first online writing circle I ever belonged to, a Yahoo group known as Channel D. They stuck by me during some very difficult times in my personal life, and I shall be forever grateful for the friendships I made there.

In my day job, I work in retail, selling products at a very large chain store in the very small town of Warsaw, Missouri. My coworkers there, and also many of our customers, have been following my writing career from its inception. I think some of them are as excited to see this book come out as I am, and I thank them for that.

Specifically, I'd like to thank Roland Davis, who believed in me when I didn't believe in myself and never let me give up.

I'd like to thank my editors at Midnight Ink, Terri Bischoff and Connie Hill, for all the hard work they've put into this book. I'd also like to thank the remarkably talented Lisa Novak for giving my story such a beautiful cover. (Isn't she awesome?)

Last, but far from least, I'd like to thank my agent, the fabulous and amazing Janet Reid. She is probably the only shark in the world who makes the water less scary for all the little writer fishes that swim in it with her.

And on a final note, Id like to thank you for reading my book. I hope that you'll enjoy it.

Loretta Ross
November, 2014

ONE

He was gorgeous and he was naked but, unfortunately, he was dead.

Wren Morgan stood in the doorway and took in the macabre sight. The Campbell house was an antebellum Victorian, the oldest house in the county. A spiral staircase rose inside a tower on the northwest corner, off the parlor. Steep, narrow steps twisted up three stories, ending at a trap door that opened into a cupola on the roof. The stranger lay draped down the bottom of the stairs, sprawled in an ungainly heap, like a discarded doll.

The hair on his head was bleach-blond, though looking at him in the all together, Wren could tell it was a dye job. He lay upside down, with his feet stretched up the steps and his head, at the bottom, twisted into an unnatural angle. Mismatched eyes stared at her unseeing, one a brilliant violet and the other simply gray. A stained glass oriel window two stories up was ajar and an early sunbeam ran down the stairs like water. Under the window, a plastic Walmart bag lay open, spilling out dark cloth. In the trees outside, a robin sang.

Gravity, acting on the blood in his body, had given the dead man one last erection.

Lying as he was, there was no way he was still alive. Still, Wren felt compelled to be certain. Crossing the dusty hardwood, she stooped to feel his throat. There was no pulse. His body was already cold and unyielding. Her fingers came away feeling slick and waxy and she scrubbed them on her jeans, fighting down bile as she retreated to the doorway to call 911.

Waiting for the police, a part of her was tempted to go out and stand in the spring sunshine. Another part, though, the part that had seen way too many horror movies, was afraid to let the dead man out of her sight. In any case, it was only a few minutes before she heard the first siren and a police cruiser squealed to a stop behind her pickup.

She heard urgent footsteps crossing the verandah and went back into the entry hall, casting nervous glances over her shoulder at the parlor, even as she opened the heavy front door. A middle-aged cop was first on the scene. It was a small town and Wren knew him by sight, but not by name. He wasn't gorgeous, but he was dressed and, thankfully, he was alive.

"You called in a report of a dead body?"

Wren tipped her head in the direction of the parlor and trailed after him as he brushed by her. She stopped at the doorway, absurdly relieved to see that the handsome corpse was still sprawled on the stairs and not lurching around among the dust sheet-covered furniture. The cop stopped in the middle of the room, not bothering to make sure the obviously dead guy was dead. He raised his radio. "This is 127, I've got a confirmation on the DB."

"Ten-four, 127."

He turned back to Wren. "Do you know him?"

"No, I've never seen him before."

He glanced around the room. "You don't live here?"

"No, Officer . . . ?"

"Grigsby."

"No, Officer Grigsby. The house has been empty for several years. The last owner left it to the Historical Society, with most of the contents to be sold at auction."

"You're with the Historical Society?"

"No, I'm with Keystone and Sons Auctioneers. It's my job to prepare the estate for sale. I came in this morning to start cataloging and appraising it."

"When's the last time you were in here?"

"This is the first time I've come. We only got the contract yesterday."

"Did you touch anything?"

Wren thought it out. "The doorknobs on both sides of the front door, the door jamb to this room, and I felt his neck."

"You felt his neck? Why?"

"For a pulse. To see if he was really dead."

Grigsby glanced up at her and she caught a glint of dark humor in his eyes. "You do realize that human heads can't turn that way, right?"

"It never hurt my dolls."

He snorted. "All right, well, we're going to need your fingerprints and you'll need to go down to headquarters and make a formal statement. You can do that this morning?" It wasn't really a question.

"Sure. We have a sale starting at ten, but I don't have to be anywhere before then."

"You're not planning on having a sale here at ten?"

"No, the Campbell estate is nowhere near ready to go to auction. Though it would be interesting to see people's faces when I start taking bids on a naked dead guy. Can't imagine I'd get too many offers."

Grigsby shook his head. "You just might be surprised about that one."

———

Death Bogart needed a win.

Death pulled his ten-year-old Jeep Grand Cherokee up in front of the East Bledsoe Ferry police station and turned to his passenger. "Okay, I'm going to come around there and uncuff you long enough for you to get out of the vehicle. I'm not in the mood to put up with any more crap from you today, so I expect you to behave yourself and come quietly. If you try to run again, you *will* be kissing the pavement. Do you understand?"

Tyrone Blount nodded once, sullen. "So what happens now?"

"You get locked up and I get paid."

Death swung down from the driver's seat and circled the vehicle to retrieve his prisoner. Blount was in his mid-forties, scrawny and flabby, with a sallow complexion. He reeked of stale cigarette smoke and sour clothes, and he was nervous and twitchy. Death had him in handcuffs, with the chain run through the chicken grip. He could read the older man's body language like a children's book, so when he reached up to unlock the cuffs, he was ready for Blount to take a swing at him and try to slip past and run away.

As soon as he was free, Blount aimed a clumsy punch at Death and launched himself from the Jeep, aiming to knock the ex-Marine down with his body weight. Death simply stepped aside, deflecting the punch and moving back in time to catch Blount by the back of his shirt and lower him to the ground. In less than three seconds, Blount was lying face-down with his hands cuffed again, this time behind his back.

Death pulled himself to his feet and stood swaying for a minute, waiting for his breathing to even out and the black spots to leave his vision. Then he dragged the would-be fugitive to his feet, frog-marched him into the police station, and turned him over to the desk sergeant.

Like the town of East Bledsoe Ferry, the police station was tiny. The cops' bullpen opened out just behind the front desk. Waiting for his body receipt, he let his gaze wander the room. It settled on a young woman who was sitting at one of the desks, filling out a form. She was pretty, in a girl-next-door kind of way, with pale skin and freckles and long, thick, red hair she wore in a single braid down her back. Whatever she was writing had her full attention. She leaned over the desk, eyes narrowed in concentration and the tip of her tongue peeking out the side of her mouth.

She wasn't really beautiful—nowhere near in Madeline's league —but Death had had his fill of beautiful people lately. The redhead looked, he thought, like someone he could get to like. He wondered if there was any chance that she might like him back.

A door at the back of the bullpen opened and a short, dark-haired young man strutted in. He wore a uniform but no gun and a simple name tag instead of a badge. A large key ring jingled at his waist. He crossed to the redhead, eyes gleaming.

"So, you finally get a guy naked and he's dead! And he was still warmer than your last boyfriend!"

The woman turned red but didn't look up. Her tongue disappeared and her lips thinned. Obviously determined to ignore him, she kept writing. The man leaned down, forearms on the desk next to her, crowding her.

"And I heard he even had a hard-on. *That's* something you've never seen before. At least he didn't have to worry you'd make his balls fall off, being as how he was already dead and all. I bet you didn't call us right away. You didn't, did you? I bet you just jumped on that bad boy and had you some cold cuts for breakfast." He wiggled his hips suggestively and made obscene grunting noises.

"Farrington!" A beefy man with a shock of white hair stuck his head out of an office. "I've got a whole drawer full of applications from people who want to work at the jail. So, if you'd rather be a standup comedian, you just let me know."

"Hey, Chief! Aw, you know you couldn't get along without me. I run that jail. I *am* that jail."

"That jail is two blocks that way. Now go."

"I'm goin'. I'm goin'."

Farrington pranced over and came out the door next to the front desk, where he stopped to examine Death disdainfully. He looked him up and down, openly sneering. "Yeah, I'm looking at you. What are you gonna do about it? Huh? Huh?" He feinted at Death like a boxer, invading his personal space, trying to make him flinch. Death just frowned down at him, bemused.

The top of the kid's head didn't clear his shoulder.

"Yeah, that's what I thought. Loser."

"*Now*, Farrington!" the chief snapped.

"Right. I'm going. I'm gone already!" Giving Death one last belligerent glare, Farrington disappeared out the door.

Death turned back to the police chief, now standing across the counter from him, reading from a sheaf of papers. "Man, what is his problem?"

"He wasn't dropped on his head enough as a child." The chief glanced up with a grimace. "He's the mayor's nephew. When he turned eighteen the fire chief and the head of the public works department and I played a hand of poker to see who got him."

"You lost?"

"I always did suck at cards. Was there something I could do for you, son?"

"Oh, uh, surety recovery agent. I brought you a skip."

"He brought in Tyrone Blount, Chief," one of the cops volunteered. "Jones's getting his body receipt." There was a crash and a muffled curse from the back. "…or possibly breaking the printer."

The chief gave Death a wry grin. "It could be a minute." He studied the younger man. "I haven't seen you around before."

"I haven't been around, and I'm pretty new to this."

"But you are licensed?"

"Yes, sir." Dutifully he produced his shiny new licenses, both of them, to save time. "Private investigation and surety recovery."

"Death? Your name is Death?"

"Yes, sir. It's pronounced 'Deeth' though."

"Like Wimsey!"

Looking up at the new voice, he found the redhead turned to face him. Her eyes were blue. A strand of hair, escaped from her braid, framed an oval face. The delighted smile she was giving him warmed him in places that he hadn't even realized had grown cold.

He grinned back at her, charmed. "Yeah! Like Wimsey!"

"Wimsey?" the police chief asked.

"Lord Peter. He was a fictional detective. In the books? Dorothy Sayers? It was his name, well, one of his names. Peter Death Bredon…" seeing a complete lack of comprehension on the cop's face,

7

he let his voice trail off. "Anyway, it's an old family name. I was named after my grandfather."

"Oh, well. Tradition's a good thing. So, Death Bogart? You know that sounds like a hero in one of my wife's bodice rippers."

"Well, I have aspired to bodice ripping. A time or two."

The redhead had completed her business and the cop she'd been talking to escorted her to the door and let her through into the lobby. She paused for a moment there, shy and blushing, clearly wanting to speak but not knowing what to say. And Death wanted her to stay, but his own voice in his head mocked him.

Hey, babe! My name's Death and I'm a penniless military reject. I live in my car. Wanna go out sometime?

He gave her a sad smile and turned away and after a minute he heard the door close behind her.

The police chief's name was Reynolds. Death read it off his name tag and filed it away for future reference. He was shuffling through a stack of pictures. Crime scene photos, Death realized.

"That the dead body the little guy was spouting off about?"

"Yeah. Nothing too sinister. He was breaking and entering and fell down a flight of stairs. We're just waiting on a fingerprint match to close the case."

Death caught a glimpse of a head shot and sucked in a quick breath. Using one finger, he pulled the picture around so he could look at it right-side-up. "Well, I'll be damned."

Reynolds looked up sharply. "You know him?"

"I know who he is. Was. Ex-con. Flow Whitaker."

"Flow?"

"Theodore really. Flow was a nickname because he was a fence and a money launderer. Cash flow? Also, it was a reference to Pretty Boy Floyd. Whitaker was a pretty boy too."

"How do you know him?"

"He's connected to a case I'm working on. So, listen. That place he was breaking into—it wouldn't happen to have been the Fairchild estate, would it?"

"The old Campbell place."

"Oh." Death frowned, disappointed.

Reynolds consulted his papers. "Belongs to the Historical Society. It was willed to them by the last owner, the late Mrs. Ava Fairchild. Campbell was her maiden name. The place had been in her family since before the Civil War. I think you'd better come back and sit down."

TWO

THE KEYSTONE SONS OF Keystone and Sons were 63, now, twins who dressed and acted so different you had to really look at them to see they were identical. Sam wore a black suit, even in the hottest weather, with a western string tie and a dusty fedora. Roy dressed in bib overalls and a plaid flannel shirt. They still did most of the calling themselves; Roy's wife, Leona, managed the business and they had sons of their own now, and grandsons even, to do the heavy lifting.

Wren had been coming to their auctions all her life and was something of a cross between a pet and a protégée. She'd been ten the first time Roy stood her on a ladder and let her sell a box of dusty baby dolls. She was a regular caller now too, and an expert appraiser. Occasionally she'd take a team of the grandsons and run an auction entirely by herself, when they had two sales at the same time.

The Melvyn estate looked to be a good sale. The goods were clean and in good repair, with modern furniture and appliances, a smattering of Depression glass, and enough antiques to draw dealers from up in the city. It was still fifteen minutes to sale time when Wren drove up and already cars packed a nearby church parking lot and lined both sides of the street for two blocks in every direction. One of the grandsons moved a sawhorse for her and she pulled into the backyard and added her pickup to the collection of battered trucks.

Crowds milled around, inspecting the wares, while the sons and older grandsons finished moving furniture into long lines on the lawn. The concession trailer was up and running, filling the air with the sharp tang of wood smoke and barbecue. Wren found Sam and Roy in the money tent, drinking soda and eating chips while Leona set up the cashbox and organized her record-keeping system.

"There's been a problem with the Campbell estate."

Leona looked up from her books, concern in her eyes. "Oh, honey! We heard. Are you all right?"

"You heard? Already?"

"Naked dead guy," Roy said. "That sort of thing tends to get around." He thought about it. "Well, actually, it's just news of that sort of thing that tends to get around. Naked dead guys don't usually go anywhere, as a rule. Not without a lot of help, anyways."

Leona gave her husband a fond, exasperated look. "Millie Weeks from the Historical Society called me. The police came around to ask her questions. They wanted to know if she knew who he was, but she didn't recognize him. She said it was a pity, though. She said that he was very handsome."

"Yeah, he was gorgeous," Wren agreed. "Plus, he was naked. Really too bad about the whole being dead thing. I'm sorry they went to Ms. Weeks about it, though. I kind of thought it should come from one of us. But I just now got done at the police station and I wanted to talk to you guys first."

"She wasn't upset," Leona said kindly. "Actually, I think she was a little thrilled to be involved in something so lurid. She's already making up ghost stories to draw in tourists when the museum opens."

"Did the police tell you anything?" Sam asked. "They figure out who he was or how he got there?"

"They think he broke in meaning to rob the place."

"Naked?"

"Yeah. He was pretty, but I guess he wasn't very smart. There's an oriel window that opens onto the spiral staircase, between the second and third floors. Well, there are several oriel windows, but this one in particular, the lock is busted. Has been for years, I guess."

"I noticed that window. But, Wren! That thing was tiny. You're not trying to tell me he got in through there."

"That's why he was naked. See, the police figure he climbed up onto the verandah roof and took all his clothes off. He put his clothes in a Walmart bag and dropped them through the window, then he coated himself with grease and forced himself inside. Tripped on the bag with his clothes in it, fell down the stairs and broke his neck."

Roy giggled and wiped his eyes. "I shouldn't laugh, but that's damn funny. Talk about your poetic justice."

"Instant karma's gonna get ya," Wren agreed.

One of the sons stuck his head in the tent. "Pop, there's a guy out here with a question about the garden tractor. Y'wanna take it?"

"Yeah, I got it." Roy pulled himself to his feet and kicked at his brother. "Come on, you old goat. Time we get this show on the road."

Sam paused to cup Wren's cheek in one hand. "You just take it easy for a bit, sweetheart. Later, if you feel like it, we'll let you call the Depression glass."

The men left. Wren got a can of soda from the big chest cooler in the corner, then sat on the chest to pop it open. She took a sip, then sighed, staring down at it unseeing as the scene at the police station played in her mind.

"You sure you're okay?"

Wren looked up, surprised to find Leona watching her out of the corner of her eye as she laid out her receipts and logbook.

"Yeah, I'm fine."

"Okay. So what are you looking all sad and humiliated about?"

Wren felt her cheeks darken. "I'm … it's nothing."

"You know I'm just going to keep bugging you. Might as well save us both the aggravation and spill it now."

That drew a rueful smile. "Eric Farrington showed up while I was at the police station. He was being … himself, I guess. He just said some really rude things."

"Huh. There's nothing wrong with the Farrington boy that a big stick and a shallow grave wouldn't solve. What did he say?"

From outside they could hear one of the brothers talking over the loudspeaker. His words were too indistinct to follow, but then he started calling and it was clear the sale had begun.

"I found a naked dead man with an erection," Wren said dryly. "Use your imagination."

"Boy's an idiot. Hell, he was home-schooled by two people who shouldn't have been allowed to breed, let alone educate. You can't let him get you down."

"Yeah, I know. Only, I was just embarrassed. And he said it in front of—" she broke off, not wanting to go there.

"In front of who? The cops? You don't need to worry about that. They know better than anyone what a little prick Eric Farrington is."

"No, not them. I … it's not important."

Leona opened a cash bag from the bank and counted out $125 dollars into a lock box, taking the paper wrapping off a bundle of ones and opening rolls of change. "Oh. I see. Was he pretty, then?"

"Who?"

"The guy you're blushing and fretting and sighing over."

"Am I really that transparent?"

"Completely."

Wren grinned. "Yes, he was very pretty. About six-one, with short, spiky, golden-brown hair and soulful, jade-green eyes. Strong Roman features, like a classical statue. Broad shoulders, narrow hips, a wide, sensuous mouth. His name was Death. And he seemed sad, but he had the nicest smile."

"He smiled at you?"

"Yes, but I think he was only being polite. I lingered on the way out, hoping to talk to him, but he just smiled and turned away." She sang the last bit to the tune of American Pie. She shrugged and her shoulders slumped. "Anyway, we both know how good I'm not at judging men. He's probably gay."

"Maybe it was a bad time. What was he doing in a police station?"

"He said he was a, um," Wren fished for the unfamiliar term, "surety recovery agent?"

"Oh!" Leona grinned. "A bounty hunter!"

"Is that what that is?"

"Mmhmm. That's the technical name for them in Missouri."

Wren giggled. "Eric was mouthing off to him, too. It was so funny! I mean! He barely came up to Death's bicep and here he is prancing around, spouting off and trying to intimidate him. Death

14

just looked at him. It reminded me of those videos you see on the web, where a big, noble Great Dane is being harassed by a chihuahua. He was like, what is this thing and why is it making that noise?"

"I wouldn't compare Eric Farrington to a chihuahua. It's cruel to insult chihuahuas that way." Leona finished her preparations, closed the cash box and turned to face Wren full on. "So, was Death The Bounty Hunter as gorgeous as Naked Dead Guy?"

"Oh, more gorgeous! Magnitudes more gorgeous. And he was living. But, unfortunately, he was dressed."

"There's just no such thing as a perfect man," Leona said wisely.

Wren raised her soda can in tribute and drank to that.

———

Most bonds, in Death's admittedly limited experience, were written for between one and five thousand dollars. Bail bondsmen tended to be very careful about securing the bonds they wrote and to keep close tabs on the people they wrote them for. When someone did cut and run, they usually went after them in person. On the rare occasions when they hired a professional surety recovery agent, they generally paid ten percent of the outstanding bond, payable upon delivery of the skip and with no expenses.

Capturing Tyrone Blount took Death almost a week and earned him $500. He traded the body receipt for a check at the bond office and made it to his bank with minutes to spare before they closed. Living as he did, time tended to get away from him. He hadn't even realized it was Saturday. Having cash in his pocket loosened the tension in his chest, but only a little.

There was no telling how long it would be before he got another skip.

He needed to gas up the Jeep and he needed real food. For three days he'd been living on peanut butter and stale protein bars he'd bought at a skiffy little thrift shop on the highway. The first thing he wanted to do, though, was rescue his gun. He'd been so broke, he'd had to hock it. Unfortunately, when he pulled into the pawn shop lot, the place was gated and dark. A sign in the front window read, "illness in family—closed until Monday."

I just have to wait until Monday, he thought, and turned away in search of a meal. It seemed that for years now his life had consisted of waiting, of trying to get by for just a few more minutes or hours or days in the hope that, if he did, everything would finally get better.

Sitting in a small diner, waiting for his meal, Death took out his phone. The Fairchild jewel case was a long shot, as lucrative and as unlikely as winning the lottery. But he had a lead now, and a reason for hope, and hope was something of which he was sorely in need.

———

Maxine Melvyn had passed away quietly at the age of 86. After picking out a few mementos they wanted to keep, her children and grandchildren had contacted Keystone and Sons. Now, virtually all of her worldly possessions were strung out across her lawn, being picked over by curious strangers.

Over the course of forty years a three-bedroom house can accumulate an astonishing array of contents. Furniture and appliances sat row upon row, interspersed with tables holding dishes, books, knickknacks, half-finished craft projects, quilt squares, board games, and practically everything else imaginable.

Sam and Roy had started at the west end of the yard, where long rolling racks were packed with clothes. The clothing was a bit of an oddity at an auction, but Maxine had been a clothes horse. Not only was her vast wardrobe in excellent condition, but it contained a lot of designer labels and there were outfits dating back to the forties, vintage clothing that would attract a whole new class of auction goers. Next to the racks, half of a long table was taken up with hats from the 1940s. Wren edged her way into the crowd around the table, breathing in the scent of mothballs and Chanel No. 5 that she always thought smelled like history.

Sam was up on the step-ladder calling and Roy was modeling the old dresses against his wiry frame. He held up a bold print dress and crowned his head with a little hat with small flowers and a dark blue veil.

"There you go," Sam said. "See? It makes him look just like Jackie Kennedy, if Jackie Kennedy had been an ugly old man."

The crowd laughed as Roy called out, "you do remember we're identical twins, right?"

Wren laughed with everyone else, shook her head and picked out a white hat to toss to him.

"Oh, sorry. My fashion consultant says this hat with this dress."

"How do we want to do this, old man?" Sam asked.

"How about choice off this rack, to start with?"

"Sounds good." Sam turned to the crowd and spoke into his microphone. "Did everyone get that? High bidder gets first pick off the rack, however many items they want at whatever the going price is each. Then we'll go from there? Okay? And-a-one-and-a-one-and-a…"

As Sam launched into his patter, Wren worked her way around the table and helped Roy hold up the various dresses. The old clothing struck a chord with her. She had a weakness for vintage and there were real poodle skirts and go-go skirts. Roy caught the look in her eye and leaned in close. "Gonna bid on something?"

She considered it. "Nah, probably not." It wasn't like she had anyone to dress up for, she thought. Her mind turned to the handsome bounty hunter again and she wondered, wistfully, if Death had someone to dress up for him.

First choice went for $73—a genuine fox fur stole from the fifties that Wren, ever the animal lover, refused to even touch. After the winning bidder claimed his prize Sam offered anyone else choice off the racks for $73 but, not surprisingly, there were no takers. On second choice it got bid up to $17. Third choice went for $10 and took out nearly two-thirds of the rack. They finished it off by selling the rest of the clothes on that rack as a lot before moving to the next one.

Sam worked his way through the racks of clothing and the half of the table that held the hats. The lower half of the table was filled with vintage dishware and when they got to it Sam shot Wren a questioning glance and she nodded and made her way up to where he was stationed.

He climbed down the stepladder and she climbed up and perched on top. "Talk fast, Wren!" Sam said into the microphone, tossing it up to her.

She caught it easily and grinned back before turning to address the crowd.

"Okay, ladies and gentlemen, we're going to move now to the dishware and knickknacks. If you look to the far end, on my right, you'll see Will holding up our first piece of Depression Glass. This is a cobalt blue Aurora creamer made by the Hazel Atlas Glass Company in the late 1930s. These were originally given out as a premium for buying cereal, but, since I don't have any cereal in my pockets this morning, I'm going to start the bidding at five dollars. AND-a-five-gotta-five-anda-six-do-I-gotta-six-anda-seven-anda-eightdoIgotta-eight-anda-nine-anda-nine-anda-gottanine-anda-ten-andadoIgotta-ten-gotta-ten-anda-half-anda-'leven-anda-half-anda-twelve-anda-half-anda-thirteen-anda-thirteen-anda-doIgottathirteen-anybodywannagimme-thirteen-going-once-anda-twice-anda-SOLD for twelve-fifty to number 23!"

Number 23 took her creamer and clasped it happily to her breast while her sister, who had been bidding against her, looked on sourly. Wren shook her head ruefully and moved on to the next piece. She had worked her way halfway through the glassware and knickknacks and was in the middle of selling a lot of horrible, big-eyed-children figurines, when she glanced up and saw Death watching her from across the crowd.

Her breath caught in her throat and she stuttered slightly and, though she caught herself quickly, she knew the brothers Keystone would have noticed her bobble and she suspected the handsome stranger had too. Nailing her attention on the bidders, she finished selling the figurines and moved on to an assortment of mismatched dishware. When she dared to glance up again several minutes later, Death was gone.

―――――

Death had to circle the block four times to find a parking place close to the auction. He got out and approached slowly—Afghanistan had made him wary of crowds—passing people leaving with boxes of books and knickknacks and an odd assortment of furniture. The scent of barbecue was already making him hungry again, but it was the sound of a woman's voice, amplified over a loudspeaker, that drew his attention. He stepped off the sidewalk to avoid a middle-aged woman possessively lugging an awkward hat rack, but then continued across the grass to where a crowd had converged around a long trestle table.

It was the redhead from the police station. She was perched on something to raise her up and was talking in a rapid-fire patter he couldn't begin to follow. Apparently she was selling something out of his line of vision. It had come down to two bidders, each trying to outlast the other, and, as she worked between them, she glanced up and caught his eye. She stuttered slightly, quickly regained her stride and turned her attention back to her work.

Death smirked, albeit sadly, and wished he were in a position to chase girls.

An old man stood to his right—a small, wizened character who still bore himself in a military fashion. He wore a sleeveless tee shirt and a denim vest with the "Keystone and Sons Auctioneers" logo on the back, and on his left arm was a familiar tattoo. An image of a bulldog, wearing a Marine helmet and smoking a cigar, appeared above a rank insignia that Death knew very well, indeed. Death nudged his arm to get his attention.

The old man gave him a questioning look and Death indicated the girl with a nod of his head. "You know her?"

He got a cool stare in return and stood patiently while the old guy looked him up and down. "She's one of us," he said, finally.

"So, tell me something. I ran into her earlier today and there was this little punk mouthing off to her. Something about never having seen a guy's junk before and making men's balls fall off?"

"Who said that?"

Death shrugged. "He was wearing a uniform. Jail guard, maybe?"

The man's eyes darkened. "Eric Farrington. That boy needs my foot up his ass!"

"Oh, I don't doubt that. It's just that, she seemed to take his nonsense to heart and I wondered if there was a story there."

"Not one that you need to know."

Death tipped his head, cajoling. "Ah, come on man. Give me a sitrep, gunny to gunny."

The other man looked him over again, this time with more interest. "Really?"

Death rolled up his own left sleeve to reveal the same insignia. He'd never been much of one for tattoos, but he'd made an exception for this. He'd gotten it when he'd known he was being discharged and that he'd never climb any higher, to always remind himself of what he had once been.

The old guy stuck out a hand. "Felix Knotty."

"Death Bogart."

"Wren's a sweet girl. I won't have anybody messing her around."

"Wouldn't dream of it."

Felix nodded, twitched his head to the side and led Death away from the crowd.

He sighed deeply. "Wren was engaged," he said. "Cameron Michaels. Writes for the paper."

"Guy was a jerk?"

"No, he was a great guy. Treated her like a princess. Sweet, thoughtful, sensitive—"

"Gay?"

"Oh, yeah! He showed up at their wedding rehearsal in a dress. Wren thought at first it was a prank, but when she laughed at him, he burst into tears. The whole thing was just sad and strange and deeply embarrassing. And, of course, this is a small town. Something like that happens, everybody knows about it."

The two men simply stood side-by-side, shaking their heads ruefully for a few seconds.

"So, you waiting to see Wren, then?" Felix asked.

Death sighed. "No, unfortunately I'm here on business, not pleasure. I'm looking for a lady named Leona Keystone."

Following Felix's vague directions, Death crossed to where a white tent sat in the corner of the yard, five or six people standing in a ragged line outside the open tent flaps. Inside, two older women sat at a folding table with a cash box and a file box between them and a large, leather-bound ledger lying to one side. Another woman leaned over the table from the front, looking at a collection of little squares of card stock.

"I got a lamp, too. I don't see that in there."

"Did you just buy it?"

"Yeah, just before I came over here."

"Hold on a second."

A towheaded kid of about twelve hurried into the tent to drop off a couple sheets of perforated card stock.

"Jody, do you see a lamp in there for number sixty-five?"

The kid glanced over the sheets, then picked one up and started breaking it into smaller squares. "Here it is. 'Big, ugly lamp, $12.'"

"It's not ugly!" Number 65 protested.

The older of the women behind the desk took the card with a roll of her eyes. "Go tell your grandfather 'no editorializing.'"

The boy grinned, grabbed a can of soda out of an ice chest in the corner and slipped away.

"That'll be forty-six dollars," the woman continued, then glanced up at Death as her customer was writing out a check. "You must be the enigmatic Mr. Bogart."

Death grinned. "I don't know about enigmatic, and I never have been called 'mister', but I am Death Bogart. Are you Mrs. Keystone?"

"We're both Mrs. Keystone. I'm Leona and this is my sister-in-law Doris."

Doris smiled up at him briefly and turned her attention to the next person in line, a tall man offering her a square of white poster board with the number 37 written on it in black magic marker.

"Millie Weeks told me to expect you," Leona said. "She said something about you wanting to look for the jewels?"

"Yes, ma'am. Um, you know about the jewels too?"

"Of course. I expect everyone around here knows about them. I just can't imagine how you hope to find them. And there's really an insurance company still interested in them? After all this time?"

Death shrugged. He'd gotten the same reaction from Millie Weeks at the Historical Society, and it puzzled him. Six years didn't seem so very long. "I guess, when a company has to pay out in a situation like that, they don't stop trying to recover their losses."

"No, I guess not. Well, Millie said the police chief put in a good word for you and the Historical Society doesn't mind you looking through the house, as long as one of us is with you. Our girl, Wren, is appraising and cataloging that lot. Why don't you get together with her? Then, when the police say it's okay to go back in, the two of you can arrange a time to meet."

"Sounds good." An excuse to spend time with a pretty lady always sounded good. "Do you know where she is?"

The boy came back, then, with another handful of sales sheets.

"Jody," Leona said, "do you know where Wren's gotten to?"

"Grandpop sent her home. Said she looked beat." He tipped his head up to look at Death. "She found a dead body this morning!"

Death caught the note of excitement and an underlying thread of envy in the boy's voice. He grinned and ruffled the kid's hair. "Some people have all the luck!"

"I know!"

He turned back to Leona. "So, um, could you tell me where—?"

"Oh no. I am not giving out a young woman's address or phone number to a strange man, and I don't care if the police chief *does* like you."

"But—"

"And you can turn on those pretty green eyes all you want. It won't change my mind." Taking a blank scrap of poster board, she wrote out an address and handed it to him. "This is where we're having a sale tomorrow. Wren will be there. You can talk to her then."

THREE

Keystone and Sons had two auctions on Sunday, the first starting at 8 AM and the second at 1 PM, so dawn found Wren in the front yard of yet another house, unpacking cardboard boxes of assorted glassware onto a long, tarp-covered trestle table. One of the grandsons plopped a box down hard, making it clink and rattle, and Wren shot him a sharp look.

"Be careful with that!" she scolded.

"Aw, it isn't anything but a bunch of crappy dishes." He took one out and held it up. "Look, the picture on it's not even clear."

"Yeah, well, it's very expensive crappy dishes. That's Blue Willow Ware from Occupied Japan, and it's worth good money."

He sighed. "Whatever."

A shadow fell across Wren's left arm. She caught a whiff of leather, a hint of aftershave, and all of a sudden Death was *right there*. He loomed over her, almost touching her, braced his lovely butt against the trestle table, crossed his arms over his chest, and leaned back to grin down at her.

"You *so* should have known!"

"Known what?"

"About your boyfriend. That he was gay. Couldn't you tell by the way he kissed you? Or even when you were making love?"

She should have kicked him in the shin and told him to get lost, but instead she found herself blushing furiously, turning away and mumbling something defensive.

"What was that?"

"He said he wanted to save himself for our wedding night."

Death hooted. "Seriously?"

"Like Superman did in Lois and Clark."

He sighed, still laughing, and shook his head. "Sweetheart, there is something you have just got to understand. Any man who's not trying to get a pretty girl like you into bed has definitely got issues!"

Wren considered that for a minute, then slanted a look up at him, sly, not raising her head. "And do you have issues?"

He laughed again at that, surprised but rueful. "Well, not *that* kind of issues, but ..." He ran one hand down his face, then straightened and scrubbed his palms against his jeans. "We've never been properly introduced. My name is Death Bogart and I'm a private investigator."

Wren took his hand. His grip was firm but not overpowering. He knew his own strength and knew how to control it. "I thought you were a surety recovery agent?"

"I have multiple personality disorder."

"I see. So what can I do for the two of you?"

He grinned again, teeth white against tanned skin. "Mrs. Keystone—Leona Keystone—said I should talk to you about searching the old Campbell place. The Historical Society has given the okay and the cops are planning to release it in the morning."

"Searching it?" She frowned. "Searching for what?"

Death shrugged. "Possibly a cache of stolen jewels."

"You mean hidden jewels."

"Well, yeah, I'd assume they were hidden."

"Yes, but you said 'stolen jewels'. They wouldn't have been stolen. I mean, of course, they might have been. But they were hidden so that they wouldn't get stolen and if they did get stolen, which, personally, I think is a very good possibility, then they wouldn't be hidden any more so there wouldn't be any point to looking for them. Because they'd be gone."

"What?" She'd spoken very fast and he shot a bewildered look at the grandson, who was still unpacking boxes on the other side of the table. The kid just shrugged.

"She's an auctioneer. What do you expect?"

"Right." Death looked down at Wren. "Could you walk that past me again?"

Wren sighed and spoke like she was addressing a small child. "You want to look for a cache of hidden jewels."

"… okay."

"What makes you think you can find them now? No one else has ever been able to."

"Yeah, well, it's a long shot, but it's worth a shot. See, the insurance company that paid off the claim would really like to recover its losses."

Now it was Wren's turn to stare. "An insurance company? Seriously? After all this time?"

"It's not really been *that* long."

"Over a hundred and fifty years?"

"Yeah. No! Wait. What?"

"What?"

They stared at each other, both bewildered.

"Just what jewels are you talking about?"

"What jewels are you talking about?"

"I asked first," Death said.

"That's childish."

"It's true."

Wren sighed. "Fine. I'm talking about the Campbell family jewels."

Death raised one eyebrow and a corner of his mouth tipped up. Wren scowled and slapped the back of her hand lightly against his hard bicep. "Not that kind of family jewels!"

"What can I say, sweetheart? That's the only kind of jewels my family ever had."

Wren scowled at him.

"Okay, okay! All jokes aside, really, what are you talking about? 'Cause I'm thinking, if there's more than one set of missing jewels, it just might explain some of the strange looks I've been getting."

She turned back to setting out dishes, both because it needed to be done and because she knew she'd never be able to concentrate on her story if she was looking at Death. "The Campbell family goes way back. They came here in the 1830s, when European settlers first began to move into western Missouri. Ezra Campbell and his wife Lydia were married in Virginia, where his family had a big plantation and a lot of slaves. Lydia was the daughter of Obadiah Healey, the artist? He did portraits and landscapes and political cartoons?" She glanced up at Death and, seeing no recognition, shrugged and continued. "They migrated here right about the time Missouri became a state, looking for cheap farmland. Their son, Andrew, married Carolina Pettigrew, the daughter of a *very* wealthy family from Natchez, Mississippi, and by the late 1850s they were living in the house here."

"You sure do know a lot about them."

"I do volunteer work for the Historical Society sometimes. I helped with the research on the house after Mrs. Fairchild left it to them." She carefully arranged a set of plates. "*Anyway*, the Civil War was harsh on the Missouri/Kansas border. Most of the towns in the area had some sort of citizens' militia and there were larger organizations, Quantrill's Raiders, for example, and the Kansas Jayhawks and the Missouri Redlegs and scores of others. Most of them claimed allegiance with one side or the other, but a lot of them were really just roving gangs, looking for any excuse to sack and loot a place. East Bledsoe Ferry wasn't a town back then, just a ferry crossing with a mill and a general store, and the Campbell estate was isolated and ripe for the picking. Andrew had gone south to fight for the Confederacy, leaving a very pregnant Carolina behind with about a dozen slaves to look after the property.

"One night they got word that a party of northern sympathizers was on the way out to free the slaves. She had them hide in the root cellar and said she'd tell the raiding party that they'd already run away."

"They did that?" Death interrupted, disbelieving. "They hid from the people who were there to help them?"

Wren shrugged. "It was a dangerous time. The armed men who claim to be there to free you might really be there to 'test your loyalty to your masters' and then punish or kill you for being willing to run away. Or they might be there to kidnap you and re-sell you somewhere else."

"Ah, I see. That sucks."

"Yeah. Anyway, it didn't work. The raiders found the slaves and took them over to Kansas, where they dumped them off in the middle of a street—this was in the winter of 1863—and basically said, 'you're emancipated. You're welcome. Now go be emancipated somewhere else.' A couple of them headed off for parts unknown, but most of them made their way back to where they started." She caught Death's look. "I guess any home's better than no home at all."

"I guess," he said, and there was an odd bleakness in his voice. "So what happened next?" he prompted.

"It took them days to get back. When they arrived, the house was dark and cold. There was ice on the inside of the parlor window. Carolina was in her bed, in hard labor, delirious with fever and bleeding heavily. One of the men went for a doctor, while the women helped her as best they could. The baby—it was a boy—survived, but Carolina died about a week later."

"And this is where the jewels come in?"

"The Campbells were wealthy. And Carolina's own family were wealthy. And, in those days, wealth meant lavish clothing and expensive jewelry. As the story goes, they had a fortune in heirloom jewelry—necklaces, bracelets, rings and earrings and tiaras and brooches and cuff links and tie tacks. Anything you could imagine, in precious metals and rare gemstones. Well, sometime between when she sent the slaves to the cellar and when they returned, it all disappeared."

"So, don't you think the marauders took it?"

"Maybe. That's certainly what everybody thought at first."

"But?"

"*But*, there was a female slave named Jenny who always told an interesting story. She said she was sitting with Carolina, trying to comfort her as she lay dying. She was holding her hand, rubbing her thumb over Carolina's fingers, and she noticed that even her wedding and engagement rings were missing. She said, 'oh, you poor thing! Those bad men took away all your pretty jewelry!' Jenny said that Carolina seemed to wake up then. She looked right at her, lucid as could be, and said, 'they didn't get it. I hid it good!' Jenny asked her where she put it, but Carolina faded back out again and didn't answer. That was the last time she seemed to know what she was talking about. She raved a lot, kept talking about 'stars in the water' and 'the seventh stone' and 'all the pretty colors', but there's no telling if any of that meant anything. And then she died. And now, a hundred and fifty years have gone by and still no one's found the missing jewelry."

Death thought about it. "She was upper crust, so probably not used to physical labor at the best of times. Plus, it was the dead of winter and she was heavily pregnant. So she wouldn't have buried it. Was there a well? Or a cistern?"

"A well *and* a cistern *and* a rain barrel. I hope you don't think that, in 150 years, you're the first to think of that!"

He grinned down at her and *damn* but he had a nice grin! "Hey, I only just heard the story and I haven't even seen the place yet. You've got to let me start somewhere!"

"Well, if you can find them, more power to you! But I thought you were looking for a different set of jewels?"

"Remember, I have multiple personalities."

Wren finished with the box she was working on and Death snagged the empty carton. "What do you do with these?"

"Put them back under the table. People will use them to carry off what they buy."

He tossed it under the table as directed, then playfully shouldered her out of the way when she reached for the next box, picked it up for her and set it down on the table with exaggerated care.

"Thank you."

"You're welcome."

"Don't think that's going to get you out of telling me your story."

"Just trying to be helpful." Death turned again to lean against the table. "My story's a lot more recent," he said. "Just as bloody and not nearly as romantic. Six years ago a masked assailant knifed a jewel courier to death in an elevator at the Royal Regency hotel in Kansas City. The courier had a briefcase chained to his wrist containing several billion dollars in both raw gemstones and finished jewelry he was delivering for a trade show in the penthouse. The killer cut off the courier's hand to get the case, stalled the elevator between floors and disappeared, apparently climbing out the emergency escape hatch on the roof and rappelling down to the basement, where he forced the doors open to get out."

"Gosh! That's horrible!"

"Yeah. They think the courier was still alive when his hand was severed."

"Oh, the poor man! And his killer got away?"

"Ah . . . sort of."

"Sort of?"

"Oh, the police know who did it. Only, they're just on the cusp of being able to prove it. All their evidence is circumstantial and it might be enough to get a conviction, but then again it might not. The DA doesn't want to risk the bastard—pardon my French—getting off, so he's not going to prosecute for now. What they really need, the one thing that would be proof positive, is the stolen jewels."

"So that's why you're looking for the jewels? So a murderer won't go unpunished?"

Death cupped her chin in his hand and turned her face up to meet his. His smile was rueful, his voice sad.

"I don't want you to think I'm a better person than I am, Wren. The insurance company that paid off after the theft has put up a

$100,000 reward for the jewels. I've had a run of hard luck lately and I'm pretty much starting over from scratch. That reward would really help me out. Plus, solving this couldn't hurt my professional reputation. I'd like to be able to be a paladin for some noble cause, and I'd love to have you see me that way. But that's not how it is and you've got to know, I'm in it for the cash."

Wren thought it over for a few seconds. "So, you can be a capitalist paladin. This is America, remember? You can be a capitalist anything."

Death laughed at that, a warm, genuine laugh. "Well, I suppose—" he said.

"But I still don't understand why you think you're gonna find your jewels at the Campbell house."

"That's because you didn't ask me who the killer is."

"Someone I know?" she asked, dismayed.

"Probably someone you've heard of, at least. Does the name Declan Fairchild ring any bells?"

"Declan? Mrs. Fairchild's nephew? By marriage. He's in prison. For ... extortion?"

"Embezzlement," Death corrected gently.

"Right. Embezzlement. Originally, she was leaving the house and everything to him. There are some second cousins and such, but he was her only close relative. But after he went to prison, she disinherited him and left everything to the Historical Society instead. He challenged the will in court, but he lost. That's why it's taken so long for the Society to get to the point of dealing with the house and getting it ready to open as a museum. They couldn't do anything until the lawsuit was settled."

"Yeah, I know. And there's more. That dead guy you found yesterday morning?"

"Yeah?"

"His name was Theodore 'Flow' Whitaker. He was a fence and a money launderer. *And* he was Declan Fairchild's cellmate in prison."

"So you think Declan hid the jewels at the old Campbell place, figuring on getting them whenever he got out of prison, because he thought that, even if his aunt died, she'd leave the property to him?"

"Right. Only she didn't leave the property to him, and when he challenged her will in court he lost. So, instead of taking the chance on someone finding his retirement fund, which, incidentally, could put him on death row, he sent his little friend in to get it."

"Only his friend was a moron and wound up dead."

"Yeah, I'm all broken up about it myself."

Wren took the last few dishes from the box on the table and had to move the empty box to make room for them. Customers were starting to congregate, picking over the merchandise. She tossed the empty box under the table with the others and tugged on Death's arm to pull him back away from the crowd.

"I don't want to rain on your parade," she said, when they were standing under a tree in relative privacy, "but has it occurred to you that the dead guy might have been looking for my jewels instead of yours? Declan could have told him the legend while they were in prison together. He wouldn't be the first person to think he could find them where everyone else had failed. Heck, right after Mrs. Fairchild died, treasure hunters sneaking in during the night practically dug up the whole yard!"

"We've already established that the Civil War jewels wouldn't have been buried."

"I never said they were smart treasure hunters," she protested, and he rewarded her with another of his gorgeous smiles.

"It hadn't occurred to me because before this morning I didn't know the other lost jewels had ever existed. Now, I suppose it's possible. But that old house is the only lead I have on my case. And, there is one more little thing, the thing that pointed me at the Campbell house even before Flow Whitaker went and broke his neck there."

"Oh?"

Death crooked a finger at her and Wren followed him to a gray Jeep Grand Cherokee that was parked at the curb. A sign on the door advertised "D. Bogart, Private Investigation and Surety Recovery."

He opened the rear, passenger-side door and took a blue cardboard folder from a net compartment on the back of the passenger seat. He opened it, extracted two sheets of paper and offered them to Wren. One was a large-scale, detailed, full-color photograph of a diamond and emerald pendant on a heavy gold chain. The other was—

"Mrs. Fairchild's obituary?"

He indicated the picture at the top of the obituary. It showed a smiling elderly lady with short, curly white hair, wearing a scoop-necked sweater and an elaborate pendant on a heavy chain. "What do you think? Is that the same necklace?"

Wren studied the two pictures. "Maybe. It's hard to tell, with the obituary picture in black-and-white. The picture quality isn't the greatest, either. This is one of the pieces from the courier robbery?"

"Yeah. Now, I'm not an expert, but I've studied them through a magnifying glass and they sure look the same to me. Oh, here." He reached back into the net pocket and offered her a large magnifying glass.

"Nice. Do you have a deerstalker hat in there too?"

"Cute."

She grinned at him, then turned to study the two pictures again through the lens. "Well, the central stone is cut the same, and they're both on the same kind of chain. A fold of her blouse is obscuring part of the setting, though, so it's impossible to really compare them. And, in black and white, you can't even tell for sure if they're the same kind of stones. If we could find the original of this picture, it'd probably be in color. Probably be larger and sharper, too."

"And that's probably somewhere in the house, you think?"

"Maybe." Wren narrowed her eyes and thought for a minute. "Or, it might be somewhere in mine."

"Yours?"

"Yeah. See, when Declan contested the will, the court issued subpoenas for a lot of Mrs. Fairchild's records and personal papers. After it was over, they returned them to the Historical Society and the Historical Society gave them to me. There's stuff in there that might come in handy when authenticating the antiques and artwork and so forth."

"Great! So, can we go look?"

Wren glanced back over her shoulder and shook her head regretfully. "Not until I get done for the day. Five maybe?"

"Really?" Death glanced around. "This is gonna last all day?"

"Well, we'll be done here about 11:30 … 12? But then we have another auction across town this afternoon. I'll probably take some of the grandsons and leave to start setting that up about ten."

"Hey, that's cool. I'm not trying to hassle you or anything. I'm just really grateful that you're willing to help me."

"I'm glad to do it. To be honest, I've been dying for my chance to search for the historic jewels anyway. Another set of missing jewels just makes it that much more exciting. And it'll be nice to have company while we're at it. So, why don't you come over about six?" She pulled a business card from her pocket, turned it over and scribbled her name, address and phone number on the back. "I'll fix some supper and we can spend the evening going through boxes. It'll be just like a children's mystery novel."

"Sounds good, Nancy Drew. So, um, I should probably let you get back to work now. And thanks again."

"No problem. See you at six, then?"

"I'll be there with my Joe Hardy hat on."

Wren went back to the auction, still being set up in the yard behind her, as Death got in his Jeep. Once she was safely hidden in the gathering crowd, she turned to watch him drive away. Then she returned to the task at hand, but with a spring in her step and a feeling like butterflies in her chest.

It's not a date! she admonished herself, but she smiled the rest of the day anyway.

FOUR

IT'S NOT A DATE, Death reminded himself. He paused at the last stop sign before turning onto Wren's street and glanced dubiously at the small bouquet in his passenger seat.

Madeline had had very definite ideas about flowers, and he wasn't really sure if her standards were hers alone or if they were shared by women everywhere. If they were, he was screwed. Madeline had expected roses, a dozen long-stemmed preferred, though half of that was acceptable if they were arranged in a lead crystal vase with greenery and baby's breath. The roses should be pink or red, and the florist's name on the box or gift card was as important as the type of flower.

Death tried to imagine, just for a second, how she would have reacted to a fistful of irises, plucked from a muddy ditch and wrapped in newspaper. He also worried a little about whether he might be insulting Wren by giving her something Madeline would have considered so far beneath her. His current finances, though, didn't run to long-stemmed roses, and he really wanted to give

Wren flowers. His mother hadn't raised him to take advantage of a woman's kindness and not at least try to repay it.

He sighed, scrubbed a hand down the side of his face and made the final turn onto a narrow, tree-lined street in a residential neighborhood at the edge of town. He pulled into the driveway behind her truck and took a minute to study his surroundings. After all these months, he still had a tendency toward hyper-vigilance. A car backfiring could send him diving for cover. But he wasn't suffering from PTSD. He told himself that on a daily basis.

Wren Morgan lived in a one-story white house with a deep, shadowed front porch, its roof supported on big, square pillars, with a rickety white picket fence around the front yard. A big red oak shaded the front. The largest branch sported a tire swing and a rut worn through the patchy grass showed it was well-used.

Death grabbed his flowers and swung down out of the Jeep. He entered the yard through a gap in the side fence and a three-legged hound dog pulled itself up and limped over to meet him.

Death stopped to rub her head and speak to her before he climbed the broad stone stair to the porch. A scruffy yellow tomcat lay like a sphinx on the left-hand plinth at the top of the stair rail. One ear was torn from fighting, a scratch ran across his nose between his eyes and his fur stood in odd spikes, a testament to old injuries long healed. Death paused beside him and the cat narrowed his eyes belligerently but suffered his ears to be scratched. Death laughed.

"You remind me of Chief McKee," he said.

"Who's Chief McKee?" Wren asked from the doorway. She wore an apron over her jeans and there was a smudge of flour across her nose.

39

"A retired Chief Petty Officer I met at the VA in Arlington. He was a Vietnam vet. A double-amputee—he lost both legs just above the knee. He had crippling arthritis, he was hard of hearing and blind in one eye. When I met him, he'd gone in to have his hand X-rayed. He punched out a twenty three-year-old college wrestler who insulted his granddaughter."

Wren laughed, a musical sound, warm with affection. "Yes, that sounds like Thomas all right."

"Thomas? Really? Not Mortimer or Methuselah or Puggsly?"

"I didn't name him," she defended herself. "The people down the street got him when he was a cute little kitten. When he got big and cantankerous, they pitched him out to fend for himself."

Death grimaced. "Gotta love people like that. What about—?" he tipped his head toward the dog.

"That's Lucy. She was like that when I found her. The vet thinks she got caught in a trap and chewed off her leg to escape."

"I see. I think you take in strays, Miss Morgan."

"There's a lot to be said for strays," she answered, and held the screen door open for him.

Death paused to wipe his feet on the mat before edging past her into a shadowy living room, already lit with the soft glow of lamps in the early evening. This wasn't a house you'd see in any magazine. Faded throw rugs were scattered across the hardwood floor. The furniture was mismatched, slightly shabby but comfortable-looking. Barn wood shelving lined the walls, holding an apparently random collection of books and DVDs and an eclectic assortment of knick-knacks.

"I, um, I brought you some flowers." Nervously, Death offered up the bouquet.

Wren's face lit up and her voice, when she spoke, was filled with warmth. "Irises! My favorite! They're beautiful! Thank you!"

He shrugged nervously, ready to apologize that they were nothing fancier, but she lifted them to her face to breathe in the scent, closing her eyes and tipping her head with delight. The purple flowers and her red hair shouldn't have gone together in the slightest, but there in the soft golden glow of the lamplight, somehow they did.

She closed the door behind him and turned to lead the way deeper into the house. "Come on into the kitchen. Dinner's almost ready. I stopped by between auctions and put a roast in the slow cooker. There's biscuits in the oven and I was just making a salad." With her hands full of flowers, she tossed her head at a high shelf over the sink that held about a dozen old odd jars and bottles. "Can you reach me down that milk bottle?"

Death fetched her the bottle and she arranged the irises with a careless flair. Cooking filled the kitchen, the richness of the roast beef and the heady smell of biscuits baking. "Is there anything I can do to help?"

"Um, yeah. Can you set the roast on the table? The stoneware insert just lifts out of the slow cooker. There's hot pads in that drawer there."

He did as she asked, setting the hot bowl on a wrought iron trivet, as she pulled the biscuits from the oven and dumped them into a napkin-lined basket. The table was already set with a selection of mismatched, colored glass dishes. The atmosphere was warm and homey and for a moment he was transported back to his mother's kitchen—tussling with Randy while Gram and Gramp and Nonna Rogers laughed at them. Dad cuffing them on the backs of their heads and telling them to use their big-boy manners.

Death swallowed hard around the lump in his throat and surreptitiously wiped his eyes.

Wren tossed the salad one last time and set it on the table and Death held her chair for her before he seated himself. He tucked his napkin into his lap.

"This is really nice," he said. "You didn't have to go to all this trouble."

"It was no trouble."

They were busy for a moment passing plates back and forth, serving themselves, buttering biscuits.

"You know, I haven't had a home-cooked meal since before I went overseas."

Wren cocked an eyebrow at him. "She didn't cook for you?"

He followed her gaze to his own left hand. The tan burned into his skin by the hot Afghanistan sun was beginning to fade, but it was still dark enough for the white circle around his ring finger to stand out in stark relief.

"You don't want to hear my sob story."

"You've obviously heard mine."

"Touché." He took a minute to eat another biscuit, thinking it out.

"You don't have to tell me if you don't want to."

Death shook his head a bit and waved his hand dismissively. "It's okay. It's just not a very interesting story. Not nearly as entertaining as finding out your fiancé's gay."

Wren frowned at him. "I'm glad everyone thinks that's entertaining. Personally, I found it more humiliating than anything."

He had the grace to look abashed. "I'm sorry," he said gently, reaching across the table to touch her hand. "You're right, and I shouldn't make fun of you. God knows, I've seen my share of humiliation, too." He pulled his hands back, scrubbed his palms against his jeans. "Madeline and I were married right out of high school. I guess she was expecting life to be all rainbows and sunshine. Heck, maybe we both were. It didn't work out that way. And, to be fair, it's never easy, being a Marine spouse. She left me while I was in Afghanistan. Cleaned out our bank account and was gone."

"I'm sorry. That sucks."

"Yeah, and that wasn't the half of it. After I was discharged, she came back broke and pregnant and wanted me to take care of her."

"What'd you do?"

"I took care of her, until her baby was born. But I didn't take her back." Death pulled together the tattered fragments of his dignity and looked Wren in the eye. "I was a Marine. The motto's 'Semper Fi', not 'Semper Doormat'."

"Good for you!"

Death gave her a small but genuine smile. "You asked if I had issues, those would be my issues."

"Everyone has issues," Wren said. "That doesn't mean ... I don't know." She tapered off, not sure if she dared say what she was thinking, but Death gave her a wistful smile and she suspected he knew what she'd left unsaid.

They topped off dinner with apple pie and ice cream, then Death helped her put away leftovers and stack their dishes in the sink. When they were ready to start going through Mrs. Fairchild's papers, Wren took an old soda bottle from the windowsill, half filled it with water and put a single iris into it to take with them into the living room.

She set the iris in the middle of the coffee table and nodded toward a closed door to one side. "There are five and a half file boxes full of papers," she said. "I've got them stacked in the corner of the bedroom."

Death gave her a wicked grin. "Are you trying to lure me into your bedroom?"

Wren blushed and scowled at him. "Do you want to see the files?"

"Of course. And your bedroom." He pushed the door open and went in, looking around curiously. Like the rest of the house, the bedroom was furnished with scarred, mismatched furniture. A sturdy wooden four-poster bed held a handmade quilt in primary colors. A huge, oval mirror topped a massive dresser and Death counted five lamps, each with a fancy shade and some sort of floral motif. The overall effect was one of character and comfort.

The file boxes were stacked in a corner off to his left. Beside them, there was a pile of plastic grocery sacks filled with old clothes. Death noticed a familiar-looking scrap of cloth and, in spite of himself, reached into one of the bags to pull out a ratty pair of men's underwear.

Wren laughed. "Scary what people will sell in a yard sale, isn't it?"

"Not as scary as the fact that you bought it."

"I didn't buy it!"

"You stole it?"

She snatched the garment from him and smacked him with it before cramming it back into the bag. "Okay, so I guess I did buy it, but not specifically." She caught the question in his eyes and explained. "On Saturdays, sometimes, I go around the yard sales when they're closing. People don't like to take things back in the house and put them away again, so a lot of times they'll let you have whatever's left for next to nothing. I wash them and mend them and then give them to the thrift shops."

"That's very public spirited of you."

She gave him a cheeky grin. "It takes a village to raise a village idiot."

Death pulled a battered baseball cap from one of the sacks and smashed it down over her head. Then he grabbed up the nearest box of files and carried it out into the living room. Wren, still wearing the cap, followed with another box.

"Do you want to just start with these and get more when we're done?"

"That's a plan." Death set his box down on the floor at one end of the coffee table and dropped onto the sofa. "You got any idea what's in these?"

"Um, not really." Wren set her box down on the table and dropped onto the other end of the couch. She glanced at Death, across the short expanse of sofa cushions, then pulled the box over to the seat between them.

Death grinned. "Removing temptation?"

"You hush."

Still laughing, Death popped the lid off of his box and pulled out a handful of papers. "I got ... phone bills. Looks like about forty years worth of phone bills. Good grief! Did this woman never throw anything away?"

"I've got a copy of the deed, some legal-ey lookin' stuff and a map." Wren turned the map sideways and then upside-down. "I can never read these," she complained. "Why is it they never put in land-marks?"

"Like what? 'Go down past the old red barn and turn left when you see a cow standing in a field?'"

"Old Man Pickering's."

"What?"

"That's how you get to Old Man Pickering's. Of course, it's a mule, not a cow, but I reckon you're a city slicker so you probably wouldn't know the difference."

"Cute. But what if you have to go somewhere farther away, like, say, Chicago?"

"That's easy. I've got a compass in my truck. Chicago's northwest, so I just drive northwest until I run into a big city."

Death grinned so big it hurt and leaned over the file box between them to whisper in her ear. "Chicago's north*east*."

Wren gave him a level glare. "I'd hit a city eventually."

"Bismarck, maybe." He took the map from her. "Hey, a plat map! This could be useful."

"Oh, I've got something else you should see, too!"

"Does it involve cleavage?" he teased as she jumped up and crossed to a bookshelf. She blushed and he laughed at her. "Just think of me as a tutorial on how to tell if a guy's gay or not. Trying to see down your shirt: straight guy."

"You're incorrigible," Wren scolded, handing him a sheaf of papers and seating herself on the floor on the other side of the coffee table.

He spread out the papers on the table. "What is this?"

"Sanbourne Insurance fire map from 1873. They put out thousands of large-scale maps of small towns in the late 1800s, to help insurance adjustors set premiums. See, the large buildings have written descriptions tagged on and it shows outbuildings, roads, wells, cisterns…"

"Where's the Campbell house?"

Wren reached across, circling a spot on the map. Death leaned in close to see. There was a muffled *pop* and the next instant every detail was sharp and clear and seemed to move in slow-motion, he could smell Wren's soap and the light, green scent of the iris between them; see the freckles on her arm and the wood grain in the table top.

Something buzzed past his cheek and the soda bottle exploded in a shower of glass and water.

Wren blinked, bewildered. Water droplets and glass shards glittered in her hair. "My flower blew up!"

Death was already in motion, diving across the coffee table. He tackled her to the ground, rolling her into the dubious cover of an old recliner and covering her with his own body.

"That was a bullet. Someone out front is shooting at us."

FIVE

Wren tucked her head into the angle of Death's neck and cringed as a second bullet buried itself in the wall behind them. She could smell his aftershave and feel both their heartbeats thudding between them.

Death made an instinctive grab at his hip and cursed softly.

"Do you have a gun in the house? I don't have mine."

"Sorry. No."

"Okay, any other kind of weapon?"

"I have an atlatl!"

He stilled and she could feel the look he was giving her. "A prehistoric spear chucker? Seriously?"

"Yeah, it's awesome. But ... probably too awkward to use indoors."

"Slightly, yeah."

From outside there was a shout. "What's going on out here?"

"How about a slingshot?" Wren offered.

"Just my car backfiring," a second voice answered.

"Where?" Death asked.

"That drawer."

"Sounds like it's about to blow up," the first voice said.

"Yeah, it's a piece of junk."

Death rolled across the floor, pulled open the drawer she indicated and found an old slingshot with a new rubber sling.

"Ammo?"

Wren took a bowl of polished river stones from an end table and slid it across the floor to him as he took up a station under the window.

"Stay there," he told her.

She hesitated only a moment before leaving the shelter of the recliner to join him.

"I thought I told you to stay there!"

"I got lonely." She raised her head just enough to see out the window. There was no screen—she'd taken it out to repair it and not put it back yet—and now the glass was shattered. She felt remarkably vulnerable without that thin barrier between her home and the outside world. A strange man stood in her front yard talking to her next door neighbor.

"Could be water in your gas. Where'd you gas up last?"

The stranger shrugged nervously and light from a streetlamp glinted off the ugly metal handgun he was hiding behind his right leg.

"Stay down," Death hissed, tugging her down to the floor. He passed her his cell. "Call 911."

"I dunno," the stranger was saying. "Murphy's?"

"They're usually okay."

"Anyway, it seems to have stopped for now."

"Yeah it does. Have you noticed any odd smells?"

"Bob's a car guy," Wren told Death.

"Never would have guessed."

Her 911 call was ringing but no one was picking up.

"Could be your catalytic converter's clogged. Is it losing power?"

Death caressed the slingshot. "You know, I haven't touched one of these since the walnut incident when I was seven."

"Rives County Authority."

"Oh, thank God! I need the police at 1731 south Locust street. There's a man with a gun in my front yard. He's already fired two bullets through the window into my house. Right now he's talking to my neighbor, who doesn't realize the man's armed."

"Who is this?"

"My name is Wren Morgan."

"Yeah, I thought that sounded like you. Now, Wren honey, I know you're desperate for a man, but the police department isn't like a Chinese restaurant. You can't just call up and order a cop to go."

"What the hell?"

Now a woman's voice joined those outside. "Bob! What are you doing out here? You're supposed to be helping me with the laundry."

"Goddammit, Eric Farrington, you listen to me! You *will* contact the real police and you *will* tell them everything I just told you and you *will* do it now or so help me, *God*, I will hang your balls from the courthouse flagpole and you may or may not be still attached to them at the time." Wren turned off Death's phone and dropped it to the floor, shaking with fury.

"Just trying to help this guy, honey. He's having car trouble."

"Well, I'm sure he's perfectly capable of fixing it himself."

"Remind me not to get on your bad side," Death grinned.

"You'd better go on," the stranger was telling Bob. "I don't want to get you in trouble with your missus."

"Yeah, I suppose," Bob agreed reluctantly. "If you need any help, just holler."

Bob retreated and a few seconds later Wren heard his screen door slam. Three heartbeats later a cautious tread sounded on the porch steps. She felt Death tense beside her, then suddenly he reared up and let fly with a rapid volley of stones. The stranger's curses mingled with Death's as he ducked back down again. Three gunshots rang through the house in rapid succession.

"I missed him! Damn!"

Next door the screen slammed open again and Bob rushed back out. "There! You see? I knew it! When a car's backfiring that bad, it don't just stop!"

"Damn it, will you get in here and leave that man's car alone?"

"Maybe you could get him while he's distracted by them," Wren suggested.

"Yeah, unless I miss. Then I'd just alert them that something's going on and he might just shoot them."

"Oh. Yeah. I don't want anyone to shoot Bob and Gina." The sound of a shrill argument rose from the yard and Wren reconsidered. "Sometimes I want someone to shoot Bob and Gina. But not for real and not right now."

Death was tossing a handful of stones up and down. "Man, my aim with this thing sucks. I didn't even come close to him. Maybe I should just tackle him now and hope I don't get shot."

Wren chewed on the inside of her cheek for a moment, indecisive, then spoke up. "Would you feel terribly insulted if I did it?"

He spun to stare at her. "Tackle him?"

"No, um, shoot him with the slingshot."

"You think you can hit him?"

"Well, it *is* my slingshot."

He considered for a bare second, then handed over the weapon and a handful of stones. "Let me distract him first and do *not* keep your head up any longer than is absolutely necessary."

He took the cap from her head and crawled over to the door. An umbrella stand there held two umbrellas, her atlatl, four six-foot long atlatl darts and her grandfather's old walking stick. Death snagged the walking stick and stuck the cap on the end of it.

Bob and Gina retreated again, raised voices diminishing with the sound of a slamming door. Death looked back over his shoulder at Wren and held up his left hand with three fingers extended. Outside, the footsteps began to once more climb the porch steps.

Death used his fingers to count down. *Three. Two. One. NOW!*

He raised the cap up to the glass in the door and it immediately exploded with another gunshot. At the same time, Wren reared up, took quick aim and let fly. Her first shot caught the gun and knocked it out of the stranger's hand. He cried out in pain and Death yanked the door open, crossed the porch in two quick strides and tackled him.

———

The porch floor shook as Death crossed it and the stranger, cradling his right hand and reaching for the gun with his left, barely had time to glance up before Death hit him. Death had a brief impression of a lean man, medium height with pasty pale skin, and then he was taking them both down the steps to the ground below.

Death landed on top, but the impact still knocked the breath out of him. He fought down rising panic at the horrible, all too familiar choking sensation that filled his chest. He swung wildly, trying to subdue the other man before he passed out, but his strength was fading and, though he landed a couple of stinging blows, it wasn't enough. The stranger pushed him off and turned on him, straddled him and wrapped long, strong fingers around Death's throat.

As the blackness closed over him, his last coherent thought was, *hell of a way to impress a pretty girl.* He was dimly aware of a sudden commotion, shouts and violence. The pressure on his neck subsided. He gasped weakly, trying to regain control of his body. There was a distant crash, and then he was being cradled in strong but gentle arms while a soft voice spoke to him, the texture of the words urgent even as their shape was drowned out by the roaring in his ears.

When the world swam back into focus, Death was lying on an orange blanket in Wren's front yard, an oxygen mask on his face and a strange man in a blue uniform bending over him, tapping him on the cheek. For one wild second he thought it was Randy and his eyes prickled with sudden tears as he remembered why that could not be.

"Take it easy," the stranger said. "Try to breathe. Can you tell me how many fingers I'm holding up?"

Death blinked and frowned. "Uh, none?"

"Oh, good. Your mind's working. For a change. Chief Reynolds tells me you're a disabled vet?"

"I'm not disabled!"

"No? Really? So, what? You just felt like taking a nap on an armed man?"

"No, I just ..."

"Passed out because you ignored the fact that you have a seriously compromised lung capacity? How bad is it?"

"It's not—" Death broke off at the look he was getting. "I'm working on it."

"Uh huh. Do you have brain damage?"

"What? No!"

"Do you want brain damage? 'Cause letting yourself get choked out would be the way to go."

"He was *shooting* at us!"

"So you went with passing out on him as a defense strategy? What were you gonna do? Gasp him into submission?"

"Man, you sound like my brother! Is it an occupational thing? To get your paramedic license you have to pass 'being a pain in the ass 101'?"

"Your brother's a paramedic?"

Death closed his eyes. "He was, yeah."

"Oh. So what's he doing now?" The paramedic read Death's silence and his voice softened. "Ah. I'm sorry." He clapped a hand to Death's shoulder. "You ready to sit up?"

Death nodded and the paramedic offered him a hand and helped him raise off the ground. The once-quiet street was chaos. Emergency vehicles crowded the narrow street, red and blue lights strobing over the houses and across the faces of people who'd come out to stare. Next door, Bob and Gina were screaming at each other again while a cop tried in vain to take their statements.

Wren sat on her porch steps, cradling Thomas, watching Death with worried eyes. The police chief stood next to her

"What happened?" Death asked. "After I, uh …"

"Went down for your nap?"

"You hush," he told the paramedic. "I was asking the chief."

"Apparently," the chief said, "your assailant started choking you, but then he ran off when Miss Morgan came out screaming at him."

"Screaming at him?"

"And I might have had a stick," Wren allowed. Death could see, now that he looked for it, a stout length of wood leaning against her knee. "I was just trying to describe his car for them."

"She thinks it may have been a Grand Am, or maybe some kind of Toyota or Mitsubishi."

Death laughed and shook his head.

"I don't do cars," she defended herself. "I know art, jewelry, books, furniture, antique toys, and glassware. I see no reason I should know cars too."

"It was a Chevelle. Mid-eighties. I didn't get a close look. Light blue."

"With a six-foot spear sticking out the back window," Wren added.

He ogled her. "You *atlatled* him?"

She glared back and raised her chin defiantly. "He shot my flower."

He gave her a cheeky grin. "It's okay, darlin'. I'll pick you another one."

One of the cops milling around was taking notes. "What's an atlally ... what you said?"

It was Chief Reynolds who answered. "An atlatl. It's a prehistoric spear launcher."

Wren held up her stick and they could see now that it was, in fact, her atlatl. It was about two feet long with a figure-eight shaped handle just off-center and a bump rising from one end. "You lay the spear along the length of the wood," she explained, "with the butt end against this bump, put your thumb and forefinger through the loops of the handle and hold the spear like a pencil. Then you bring it up and over like you're throwing a baseball. The spear tip rises up as your arm comes forward and the back end of the atlatl pushes the spear off. It's just simple leverage, really. With practice, you can throw a spear up to ninety miles an hour."

"They're legal for hunting in Missouri now," the chief threw in. "Not Chevelles usually. You don't seem like the hunting type. How is it you happen to have one?"

"It was in an auction we did once and I thought it looked interesting. It's just for target practice."

"Like the slingshot?" Death asked.

"Sort of. I mainly bought the slingshot so Mrs. Winters wouldn't buy it for her son Miles."

"Wise move." Reynolds crouched down to Death's level. "Wren didn't get a good look at the shooter. Did you?"

"Real quick one." Death chewed on his lower lip. "If I didn't know better, I'd think it was Declan Fairchild."

"Probably was then."

"But isn't he in prison?" Wren objected.

"He was. He walked away from a trustee work release program early this morning."

"When did Whitaker's name hit the news?" Death asked.

"It was in the local papers this morning."

"He made the 'odd news' section at several online sites, too," one of the cops offered.

"Why was he a trustee?" Wren demanded. "I mean, didn't you tell me he cut a man's hand off and then killed him?"

Death pushed off the ground and tottered over to sit next to her on the steps. "He's never been charged with that. The only thing he's been convicted of is a nonviolent, white-collar crime."

"Well he doesn't seem very nonviolent to me. And why shoot at us? I've never even met the man, have you?"

"No. He might have heard that I'm looking for the jewels, I guess, but would that be enough to make him come after me? And how would he have even known where I was?"

Death could feel her trembling beside him. "Don't worry. I'm not gonna let him hurt you."

Chief Reynolds considered this. "You didn't shoot back," he said.

Death felt the heat rise in his face under Wren's gaze and that of the Chief and his officers. "No, I, uh, don't have my gun with me." They waited, silent, and he ducked his head in shame. "I hocked it a few days ago. I went to get it back yesterday, but the pawn shop was closed until Monday."

Reynolds nodded to himself, pulled his backup piece, checked the safety, and passed it to Death butt-first.

"You're lending me your gun?"

"Just until you get your own back tomorrow."

Humbled, Death took the gun with an awkward nod. "Thank you. I don't know what to say."

"I did a background check on you. I don't just know that your lungs are messed up, I know how they got that way. You can just give that gun back tomorrow."

"Why was Eric Farrington answering 911 calls?" Wren asked. Death shot her a quick look, grateful for the change of topic.

"He wasn't," the chief said. "A technician working on the phones accidentally routed one of the 911 lines to the jail. Eric tells me you threatened to cut his balls off, by the way. I told him not to worry. If anyone really believed he had any balls, they'd have cut them off years ago."

Death snickered, then regretted it as it triggered a coughing fit that had black spots dancing in front of his eyes again.

The chief pounded him on the back until he could breath, then turned his attention to Wren. "I doubt Fairchild will be back anytime soon. He'll have to know that we're going to be watching your house now. But if he does come back, we'll get him."

"Unless," Death added, "you atlatl him first."

SIX

A LOUD *BANG* JOLTED Wren awake with a painful gasp and a tight knot of terror in her chest.

"Screen door next door."

Death's voice was calm, but she was lying with her head against his arm and she could feel his heart beating like a trip hammer.

"Are you sure?"

"I'm sure."

They lay side by side on top of Wren's bed, both clad in sweats, Chief Reynold's gun within easy reach on the nightstand. There hadn't been any real discussion about Death staying the night. It just happened. The police dug the bullets out of her living room walls and nailed sheets of old plywood over the shattered front window and the window in the door. Death had showered and changed while there were still cops obvious in the yard, then he'd stood guard at the bathroom door while she did the same.

"Are we still going back to the Campbell place this morning?" she asked.

"Do you still want to? I'll understand if you're afraid."

"No, I want to. I'm not letting that ... that ..."

"Scumbag?" Death suggested. "Weasel? Scoundrel? Creep?"

"I was thinking more along the lines of 'son of a bitch.'"

Death sat up and grinned down at her.

"Son of a bitch works for me."

"Okay, so, I'm not letting that son of a bitch control me. How about we have some breakfast and then go see if we can't find ourselves some jewels?"

———

"Is your truck running okay?"

Death was riding to the Campbell place in Wren's truck and he frowned and leaned over, trying to see the gauges.

"Why?" she asked, instantly panicked. "Do you hear a funny noise? Is it shimmying or bobbling? Do you smell antifreeze or burning or something?"

"No, it's just that we're barely moving."

She frowned over at him. "It's going as fast as I always go."

He raised his eyebrows. "You mean you're driving like this on purpose?"

"What's that supposed to mean? I'm doing almost the speed limit, you know."

"Huh. You drive like a little old lady."

"How do you think they get to *be* little old ladies?"

"Cute. Well, I'm gonna be a little old man by the time we get anywhere."

She shot him a sly, sideways glance. "So, you're saying that you're a little man?"

"Oh, no!" He raised his hand and wagged a finger at her as she cackled at him. "You did not even go there."

They stopped first at the pawn shop to ransom Death's gun, then went to the police station to return the Chief's. There was little new information on Declan Fairchild. The Chevelle had been stolen from a used car lot and had turned up abandoned in the next town over, atlatl dart still embedded in the back window.

"Just for the record," Reynolds asked, "why did you feel the need to throw a spear at him. He was already driving away, wasn't he?"

"I wanted to encourage him to not come back."

The Campbell house and property took up almost an entire block. Death made Wren circle it twice before she pulled into the driveway.

Death grinned and looked down at her. "Remind me," he said, "am I protecting you today or are you protecting me?"

"We're protecting each other."

"You're unarmed."

"I have my slingshot hidden in my bra," she said, and then leaned away when he tried to see.

"Why didn't you bring your atlatl?"

"My bra's not that big."

He laughed out loud at that, swinging down from the truck, loose and carefree and yet watching, always watching, looking for movement in the shadows and securing the perimeter.

Wren came around the truck with a set of keys at the ready and he followed her onto the porch, peering through the windows into the dim interior. When he was satisfied the coast was clear he nodded to her. She unlocked the big front door and he guarded her back and allowed her to lead the way inside.

"You know, the last time I was here was when I found the dead body."

"Yeah. Try not to do that anymore."

The front door opened into a massive formal entry hall.

"This room is a perfect cube," Wren said. "It's sixteen feet square and sixteen feet tall. The staircase is made from Virginia oak that was shipped by barge up the Mississippi and then across on the Missouri to Independence, where it was transferred to horse-drawn wagons for the remainder of the journey."

"Not by train?"

"The railroads didn't come this far west yet."

"I see. And is Virginia oak really that much better than Missouri oak?"

"They apparently thought so. If nothing else, having to ship it would have made it outrageously expensive. That would have been a bragging point. I think the wood for the parquet floors came from Virginia too."

Even in the dim light and under a heavy coat of dust, the wood floors gleamed. Police tracks criss-crossed it, the overall sense of disorder a nagging itch at Death's military soul. He wanted to go find a private and make him clean it. The Virginia oak staircase rose from the center of the room, met a landing six feet up the back wall and divided into two smaller stairs that climbed left and right to a mezzanine that circled the hall on the second floor.

Dust sheets covered everything, from sparse groups of furniture that Death suspected were more for show than for use to the framed pictures covering the walls.

Wren began pointing out doorways, beginning on their left. "There's the sitting room, then the morning room, then the formal dining room. The kitchen is down that hall at the back. It's actually a converted housekeeper's sitting room. The original kitchen was in a separate building out the back. That way, if it caught fire, it wouldn't burn the whole place down. There's also a pantry and some other utility rooms down there. Oh, and the bathroom, if you need it. The Historical Society got the lights and water turned on again."

"That was considerate of them."

"Well, as soon as we get done with the auction they're going to start working in here anyway, getting it ready to open as a museum." She half turned and indicated the doors on their right. "The study is at the back, then the library, then the parlor. The tower opens into the parlor and that's where I found the naked dead guy." She hesitated for a minute, chewing her lower lip. "I don't suppose you'd like to go make sure that he's gone, would you?"

Death laughed. "The cops took the body away two days ago!"

"Yeah. And your point is?"

He chucked her on the nose, walked past and checked the parlor. "Yup, no naked dead guys here. Though there could be a naked live guy, if you think you'd like that."

Her face turned red and she glanced away, embarrassed. "You're incorrigible!"

"Think of it as a teachable moment. Guy offers to take his clothes off for you: Straight guy."

She stuck out her tongue at him and took a firmer hold on her notebook. "So. Where do we start?"

"What would you normally do? What were you doing when you found the naked dead guy?"

"I was walking around looking at everything going, 'dang! Where do I start?'"

Death laughed. "Let me re-phrase that. What is it you need to do for the auction?"

"I need to make a list of everything in here, then track down the provenance on everything I can. Then we'll take the list to the Historical Society and they'll decide what pieces they want to keep for display and what pieces they want to sell. It's going to take a long time to prepare this auction, but when it happens it'll be huge. Not only is there a lot of stuff in the rooms, but the attic and two of the outbuildings are crammed too. Sam and Roy looked it over when they put in the bid to do the auction and they think it's a hodge-podge of things ranging from priceless antiques to plain old junk."

"So maybe clear the house first, then the attic and then the outbuildings?"

"Yeah. When we get to the attic and outbuildings I'll conscript some of the grandsons to come do the lifting."

"The grandsons?"

"Keystone Auctioneers is a family business. Originally it was Roy and Sam and their dad. Now it's them and their sons and grandsons." She looked around again. "Why don't we start with the furniture?"

Death started pulling the dust sheets from the furniture. Wren watched him, frowning slightly and chewing on her lower lip.

"What's the matter?"

"You know, you don't have to help me. I know you're really here to look for the jewels."

"Right. But the best way for me to do that, I think, is to get a feel for the house. Helping you is as good a way to do that as anything."

Wren nodded, but still didn't look happy. After a minute, Death set aside his armload of dust sheets and went over to cup her cheek in his palm.

"I'm not going to pass out on you again."

"Promise?"

"I promise."

She sighed and nodded and followed him back to the door. He'd uncovered a chunky wooden combination hat rack/umbrella stand and she photographed it and recorded the pictures in her spiral notebook. He searched through the compartments, not really expecting to find anything but wanting to be thorough. Wren was still uneasy, working her way up to asking him something, and he waited patiently.

"Death?"

"Mmm?"

"Would you tell me what happened to your lungs?"

"You didn't get the story from Chief Reynolds?"

"No. I tried, but he said I should ask you. He just said that you're a good man."

Death ducked his head, more embarrassed by praise than he would have been by censure. "It was in Afghanistan. I was wounded in action." He stopped there, but she only waited in silence so after a moment he went on. "Hummer we were riding in hit an IED, then came under fire from insurgents. I had three guys with me. We were all banged up to some extent, but I got two of them out and under cover. Our driver, though was trapped behind the steering wheel. I went back for him and got him free, but we barely made it clear of the vehicle before it took a direct hit and exploded. I took a chest full of shrapnel. Everybody thought we'd been killed when the Hummer went up, and we had to hide out in a dirty cellar for three days before we were able to contact U.N. forces. My injuries got infected and I wound up with double pneumonia and a collapsed lung."

He stopped and grinned down at Wren, who was watching him with tears in her eyes. "I got all my guys out. They're all okay now."

Wren sniffled and wiped her eyes with the back of her hand. "I think the chief was right," she said.

It took all morning to work their way from room to room on the first floor, uncovering and documenting furniture. Wren was obviously reluctant to go back into the parlor and Death tried to tease her out of it. Finally, as noon approached, they had nowhere else to go unless they wanted to move up to the second floor. Death caught Wren eying the staircase longingly and took her shoulders.

"Hey. I know you're not real anxious to go back in the parlor, but the more you put it off, the worse it's going to be. I already checked it, remember? No more naked dead guys, I promise."

She hesitated. "Did it smell … funny?"

"Funny like a clown?"

She smacked his arm, hard.

"Ow! Hey, wounded warrior here, remember?"

She rolled her eyes and he grinned down at her. "Okay, sorry. No, it didn't smell like anything but dust. I promise. The body wasn't there long enough."

Wren looked doubtful but finally followed him into the parlor, half hiding behind him and sniffing cautiously. Once they stood in the center of the room, she finally relaxed and moved away.

"This is a nice room, as long as there's no dead guy here."

"Yeah, it's bright. Got a nice feel to it."

"A lot of hiding places," she suggested. "I've always thought the Civil War jewels were probably hidden in some secret compartment built into the walls or something. Maybe they could be in here."

"Maybe." Death let his doubts creep into his tone.

"You don't think so?"

"What happened to Carolina's husband? You said he was away fighting for the Confederacy. Did he survive the war?"

"Yeah, he lived to be in his nineties."

"And you're sure he never found the jewels? If he was a Southern sympathizer, his fortunes probably went downhill after the war was over. Maybe he sold the jewels and was just too proud to let anyone know."

"No, we know he didn't find them because he spent the rest of his life looking for them. In 1872 he even had a big party where he invited everyone in to try to help him find them. He re-married that year and wanted to give them to his new bride. Of course, that started a bunch of ghost stories about Carolina guarding the jewels because she didn't want another woman wearing them."

Here in the dust and sunshine the room had a pensive air. Standing in a home that had outlived its family in all their generations, Death could well believe there were ghost stories, and maybe more than stories even. He didn't think he'd like this mansion nearly so well in darkness, even without a naked dead guy.

"Huh. Well, okay, then. If he didn't find the jewels, then they weren't in any kind of secret compartment in the walls."

"How do you know?"

"His family built this house. If there were secret compartments, he'd have known about them."

Wren smacked herself in the forehead. "How come I never thought of that? It sounds so obvious when you point it out."

"Well, I am the detective."

She started to say something, doubtless some clever comeback, but something else caught her attention.

"Hey! What's that?" She darted across the room, stooped beside a covered chair and came up with a thin, translucent violet disc. "What is it? It looks kind of amethyst-ey. Could it be something off one of the pieces of jewelry? It's so tiny!"

Death grinned. "Hey! Good job! You found Flow Whitaker's missing contact lens!"

She stared at him.

"What?"

"Flow Whitaker? Naked Dead Guy? He was wearing colored contact lenses. One of them was missing. The police looked for it but, no luck. We'll have to tell them you found it."

She shrieked and flicked her fingers, flinging it across the room.

"…and lost it again."

"Ewww! Ewww! That's disgusting! How could you let me touch that thing?" She wiped her fingers on his shirt and he wiggled away, laughing as it tickled.

"It's okay. It was just a contact lens!"

"It was a dead guy's contact lens! It was in his eye! It was in his dead eye! Ewww!"

"It's not like he was contagious. Stupidity is not catching, I promise. Neither are broken necks. Look, I'll prove it to you. You take your clothes off and I'll catch you when you climb in the window."

Wren glared.

"See?" he asked. "Guy trying to get you naked: straight guy."

She hit him again and stormed off in the direction of the bathroom. Laughing, Death wandered over in the general direction Wren had thrown the contact lens. It only took him a minute to spot it again. Light coming in the windows over the staircase made it shine against the dark wood of the fourth stair from the bottom. He leaned over to pick it up and froze.

The riser between the fourth and fifth stair had been removed, exposing a dark, empty recess under the fifth step. His first sick thought was that he was too late—Fairchild had gotten the jewels and gone. But then he realized that the thick layer of dust inside the hiding place lay undisturbed except for one clear hand print in the middle.

He heard Wren come into the parlor behind him. She must have read something in his posture.

"Did you find something?"

"You could say that." He straightened and turned to face her. "I know why Declan Fairchild came after you last night."

"After me. You think he was after me?"

"Yeah. He came here first and found his stash of jewels was missing. He must think that you're the one who took them."

SEVEN

The Paper Pagoda Chinese restaurant was housed in an old, red, wood-frame building set on a rocky promontory, hard by the east end of the swinging bridge. Wide decks, built up on stilts, surrounded it on three sides, hanging out over the swift currents of the upper Osage. It had always reminded Wren of a houseboat on the river.

Wren sat inside in a booth now, watching out the window as rain drops spattered on abandoned patio furniture. A bright morning had given way to a blowsy, blustery noontide, with the promise of real storms in the thunder rumbling across the water.

The radio was tuned to the local station and the announcer was giving the noon news.

"In East Bledsoe Ferry this morning, police say there has been a second break-in at the old Campbell house, just two days after an intruder died in a fall down the house's spiral staircase. Police Chief Duncan Reynolds said that two employees of Keystone and Sons

Auctioneers, who were working in the house, discovered a secret compartment, open and empty."

The police chief's voice came over the radio. "We don't believe anything was actually taken. It's obvious from the amount of dust in the compartment that if anything was hidden there, it was removed years ago."

The announcer resumed. "That was East Bledsoe Ferry Police Chief Duncan Reynolds. The old Campbell house, now the property of the Rives County Historical Society, is the site of a famous local story concerning jewels that disappeared during the Civil War. Historical Society President Millie Weeks discounts the possibility that the jewels are still hidden somewhere in or around the old house."

Millie Weeks's voice was cultured and smooth, with a light Southern accent. "The rumors that there is a hidden treasure there hinge on the fevered ravings of a dying woman. The house and grounds have been searched repeatedly over the past century and a half with no result. We believe that it's most likely the jewels were stolen back in 1863 by the very marauders they were supposedly hidden from."

"Ms. Weeks intimidates me," Wren said. "She reminds me of my grade-school principal."

Death, seated across from her, made a rude noise and shook his head. "You can't be intimidated. You throw atlatls at people."

"Technically, I throw atlatl darts at people. You don't want to throw the actual atlatl. You can always threaten to hit people with it, though."

"There, you see?"

"Wren?"

Wren looked up at the man who'd approached their table. "Cam?"

Any passion she'd ever felt for him was gone now, but the love was still there, tempered to something more sisterly. He was tall and slender, perfectly dressed and groomed, as always, gentle and sensitive and impossibly sweet. Seeing him next to Death, who was undeniably masculine, it was harder than ever to understand how she hadn't guessed earlier that she really wasn't his type.

Oh, God, she hoped Death didn't launch into any of his jokes!

"Cam?" Death said. "As in Cameron Michaels?" He stood and offered Cam his hand. "Wren's told me about you. Like to join us?"

Cam agreed and Wren slid over to make room for him on her side of the table. The idea of him sitting next to Death was just too weird for her to contemplate.

"I heard there was another break in at the Campbell house," he said. "This is just unbelievable! Do you know we got another dead body this morning? We go years without any dead bodies at all and now we get two in just three days!" He grinned self-consciously. "It's probably not seemly for me to be so excited, is it?"

"Reporters," Death grinned. "So what happened? Accident? Suicide?"

"No, he was murdered! Somebody stabbed him, like seventeen times!"

"Declan Fairchild?" Wren asked, unhappy at the thought.

"Oh, no, sweetie," Cam assured her. "Fairchild just broke out of jail yesterday morning. This guy had been dead awhile. He was pretty ripe, I'm sorry to say."

"What about Whitaker? Would he have killed someone?"

"Not that way," Death answered. "He was a pansy."

Wren felt Cam stiffen beside her. "You mean he was gay," he said, voice level.

"No, I mean he was a pansy." Death smiled a crooked grin that made Wren's heart beat a little faster. "When I was in the Corps there was a gay Marine in my squad. Let me tell you, he was *nobody's* pansy. I don't know what Whitaker's sexual orientation was, but I do know he was conceited and prissy. You stab someone, there's gonna be a lotta blood. You're gonna get it all over you, and you're gonna have to get close enough to them that they might be able to claw you up in self-defense. If Whitaker had decided to kill somebody he'd have shot them or poisoned them. Nothing hands-on."

"That makes sense," Cam admitted.

"Death's a pretty smart guy," Wren said, half-teasing.

"Yeah," Cam agreed. "Pretty and smart. I think you should keep him."

Wren felt her cheeks flame, and changed the subject. "So, Mr. Smart Guy, if Fairchild and Whitaker are innocent, who do you think killed the new dead guy?"

"How should I know?" Death protested. "I don't even know who got killed."

"Oh, didn't I say? It was an old man named Josiah Halftree. He was a jeweler down at Cold Spring."

"Really?" Death's interest was suddenly sharp, catching Wren's attention and Cameron's too.

"That means something to you? Why?"

Death thought about it. "Off the record?"

"I hate those words!" Cam complained.

Death just stared at him, patient and stern.

"Okay, fine. Off the record."

"Okay, well," Death looked to Wren, "after you went to sleep last night, I sat up for a while, reading through some more of Mrs.

Fairchild's papers. She had several letters from Josiah Halftree. I remember it because of the unusual name."

"Did she? Really? What were they about?"

"Nothing out of the ordinary. Pricing information on an engraved, sterling silver christening bowl, a notice that her watch was fixed and ready, something about her engagement ring being cleaned."

"That doesn't necessarily mean anything," Cam said, disappointed.

"No, no it doesn't. It's provocative, though, isn't it?"

They had finished eating before Cam arrived. Now they sat in companionable silence. Death cracked open his fortune cookie and glanced at the slip of paper inside before balling it up and fiddling with it restlessly.

"Oh, my God!" Cameron exclaimed suddenly. "You guys got shot at last night! I almost forgot. You see? Any other time an armed assault would be the biggest news to hit this town in a month of Sundays. But now, between two dead bodies and another intruder at the Campbell house, I forgot all about it."

"Yeah, I was a little surprised you didn't show up last night," Wren admitted.

"I was covering the high school baseball game over at Thibeaux Crossing and I didn't hear about it. The game went into overtime and by the time we got back, it was all over."

"Oh. How'd we do?"

"Well, you must have done okay, you're both still here."

"No, I meant in the baseball game."

"Oh. We lost. Three to one in eleven innings."

"Dang."

"Yeah."

"So, you're with the paper, right?" Death asked thoughtfully.

"He practically *is* the paper," Wren said, while Cam just nodded.

"Right. So, I don't suppose you guys'd still have a copy of the picture that was used for Ava Fairchild's obituary, would you?"

"Possibly." Cam thought about it. "Probably. Normally, we'd return the original to the family, but Mrs. Fairchild didn't really have any family. You know, it seems to me that we had trouble even getting an obituary picture."

"You remember an obituary from four years ago?" Death asked.

"Small town. Important lady. She was the last direct descendant of the family that pretty much built this town. If I remember rightly, there was a cousin or something who had a key to the mansion and he let us in to look for a picture, but we couldn't find anything more recent than when her husband was alive. He died nearly thirty years ago."

"So what did you do?"

"I don't remember."

"What would you do now, if you ran into the same sort of problem?"

"I guess the first thing would be to look in our own files and see if we had ever taken a picture of her that we could use."

"Could you do that again? Maybe it's in there?"

"Yeah, ok ... Sure. Can I ask why?"

"Just following up a hunch. I'll tell you if it pans out. I promise."

He grinned another of his irresistible grins and Wren felt Cam half sigh next to her. "You don't happen to have a gay brother, by any chance?"

Death's smile was wry and sad. "No, 'fraid not."

"Yeah, that figures." Cam's smile was wistful. "Anyway, I'm glad that Wren's going to have you around. Especially if people are going to keep shooting at her." He switched his attention to Wren. "Are people going to keep shooting at you?"

"Well, I hope not!"

"That was the reason Chief Reynolds released the story about the hidden compartment." Death explained. "We're hoping that Fairchild will hear it and realize that Wren can't be the one who took the jewels. But if he does come back, I'll be there. Don't worry."

"I'm glad you're taking care of her." Cam sighed. "I was never very good at that."

"Hey," Death said, "you did the right thing. I know it can't have been easy and I know there are probably times you think you should have just kept on pretending and gone on with a 'normal' life. But Wren could never make you happy, no matter how hard she tried. And you could never really make her happy, no matter how badly you wanted to. If you're going to love someone and spend the rest of your life with them, then it's important to be true to them, right?"

Cam and Wren both nodded.

"Right. And you can never be true to another person until you first learn to be true to yourself."

"Gosh," Cam said. "Wow. Gee, that's ... really, *really* a cool thing for you to say. I don't ... I don't know how to respond to that. Thank you. Thanks. I," he glanced at his watch, "I've got to run. I'm on deadline. I'll look into the picture thing and get back to you. It was really great to meet you." He offered Death his hand and Death shook it.

"Glad to meet you."

"Wren, honey, you take care. Call me if you need anything." Flustered but pleased, Cam slid out of the booth and took his leave.

As Wren and Death got up to leave as well, she touched his arm.

"That was such a cool thing for you to say. Cam has had a really rough time of it since he came out. What you said, it was just so sensitive and so … *profound*."

He gave her a cocky grin. "Yeah, baby, that's me. Sensitive and profound." He lobbed a tiny wad of paper in her face and she caught it startled. As he pulled out his wallet and headed for the cash register, she smoothed out the little ball and found it to be the fortune out of his fortune cookie.

Before you can be true to another, it said, *you must first learn to be true to yourself.*

———

The rain fell harder, soaking Death's shoulders and running down the back of his neck as he stood at the edge of the Paper Pagoda's deck, waiting for Wren to come out of the ladies' room. He'd moved his Jeep around so the passenger door was as close to the restaurant as he could get it. Now he was standing guard, watching the highway and scanning the bushes and the footpath leading to the old swinging bridge.

It would be a shame to survive Afghanistan, he thought, *only to get shot in East Bledsoe Ferry.*

Wren came out, ducking her head against the rain, and he met her, rushed her to the Jeep and opened the door for her. When she was safely inside, he circled and climbed in beside her, shaking water droplets from his short hair.

"Did you call the Chief and tell him about the letters from Mr. Halftree?" she asked.

"Yeah. You wanna hear something else provocative? One of the last people to talk to Josiah Halftree was Millie Weeks."

"Ms. Weeks? She wouldn't stab anyone! Flay them, maybe, but only if they put an extra 's' in business or pronounced 'library' without the first 'r'."

"Well, maybe she was trying to flay him and she just got careless."

"Ms. Weeks would *never* get careless."

"Why don't we go ask her about him anyway?" Death caught the uncertain, half-fearful look she shot him and laughed. "You can hide behind me if you really want to."

"If her mother's there, you might want to hide behind me. She'll try to pinch your butt."

"Her mother? The Ms. Weeks I talked to was, like, seventy!"

"Her mother's ninety-seven. She'll try to pinch your butt. Cameron says she's got a grip like a crawdad. The Keystone twins won't go within a mile of her."

"Huh." Death considered. "You still got your slingshot in your bra?"

"Of course."

"Well, all right, then. Let's go."

The two Ms. Weeks lived in a quaint little stone cottage in the midst of what Wren claimed was a classic English garden. To Death it pretty much looked like flowery weeds, but he was wise enough not to say so. Millie Weeks met them at the door and ushered them into a cozy living room crowded with antique furniture, throw pillows, and knickknacks, many of them of the "hideous big-eyed children" variety. In the dim lighting, Death didn't realize that the wizened old doll sitting in a corner rocking chair was alive until Mother Weeks had latched onto his backside.

Cameron was right.

"Mother!" Millie Weeks snapped. Her mother let go, but gave Death a toothless and entirely unapologetic grin.

"I am so sorry!" her daughter apologized. "Why don't you come sit over here? Would you like me to get you an ice pack or something?"

"No. No, thanks. I'm good." He glared at Wren and got a small shrug back.

"Sorry. I didn't see her either."

"You want my advice, girlie?" Mother Weeks piped up, looking at Wren. "Pinch butts now while you're young and cute. No one appreciates it when you get to be my age."

"Thanks, Mother Weeks. I'll keep that in mind." Wren grinned at her and gave Death a sideways, speculative look.

"Don't start something you're not prepared to finish," he growled softly, for her ears only, and was pleased to see her blush a fiery red in response.

Ms. Weeks offered them tea or coffee, which they declined, then sat across from them in a wooden rocker and sighed sadly. "So I suppose this means the jewels are gone? The ones from the robbery in Kansas City?"

"You know about that?" Wren asked. "I understand there was some confusion at first."

"Yes, there was, but Chief Reynolds explained it to me after Declan Fairchild shot at you last night. He was concerned he might come after some of the Historical Society members and wanted to warn us to be extra careful."

"Damn," Death said. "I'm sorry. I should have thought of that."

"I don't see why. That's what we pay him for. Anyway, no one's seen anything so far, so no harm, no foul. It's just a shame about the jewels."

"I'm not so sure they are gone," Death said. "I'd like to keep looking, in any case, if that's all right with you."

"It's fine with me, but why do you think they might not be gone?"

"Well, they haven't turned up on the market or I'd have heard about it. Plus, I've kind of got a hunch about what happened to them."

"You do?" Wren exclaimed. "Why didn't you say anything?"

"I wanted to wait and see if it panned out first. You know, the less you say, the smarter you sound."

"Is that another fortune cookie?" she asked sourly.

He gave her a cheeky grin. "It could be." He turned back to Ms. Weeks. "What I was hoping to ask you is, what were you talking to Josiah Halftree about? If you don't mind telling me. The Chief said you were one of the last people to speak to him."

"So I understand. Poor man. I didn't see him in person, you know. He phoned me last Wednesday, the day we closed bids for someone to handle the Campbell house auction. He wanted to suggest to me that the family jewels should be handled separately by a professional jeweler—himself, of course. Only there were no jewels to speak of among the things we got. Some obvious costume jewelry and a few little pieces that we already had valued and that weren't worth anything. But Mr. Halftree was just certain that Ava Fairchild had had some very valuable jewelry in her estate."

"Did he say why he thought that?"

"He said that he'd seen it."

"What did you tell him?"

"Well, we didn't get everything from her estate. There were a few isolated bequests to friends and family members. I suggested that maybe one of them had inherited the jewelry."

"I think you'll find that they didn't," Death said, "but it was a good thought." He turned to Wren. "It's really starting to pour out there. If it's okay with you, I'd like to see you safe at home before the streets flood."

"Of course." He and Wren stood to leave.

"But aren't you going to tell us your theory about the jewels?" Ms. Weeks asked.

"Let me see if it's right or not, first," he hedged. "When I know, I'll tell you, even if it's to tell you I was wrong."

They said goodnight to Mother Weeks, Death carefully keeping his distance, then Ms. Weeks showed them to the door. A quick dash through the driving rain, and they were safe in Death's Jeep once more.

"Will you tell me?" Wren asked.

He started the engine and sat for a moment, letting the heater warm them up and pull steam from their sodden clothes. "When did Mrs. Fairchild disinherit Declan?" he asked. "Was it when he was sent to prison?"

"No, I think she supported him at first. But then, just a few months before she died, she had a change of heart and wrote him out of her will. That was the gist of his lawsuit. He claimed the Historical Society ladies had used undue influence on a senile old woman."

"She wasn't senile."

"What do you think happened?"

"I think Ava Fairchild found the jewels hidden under the stairs. I think she thought at first that they were the Civil War jewels, but when she took them to a jeweler—"

"Josiah Halftree?"

"Josiah Halftree. She took them to him and he told her they were too modern to be from the 1800s. That's when she realized where they had to have come from and what they had to mean—that her nephew wasn't just an embezzler, he was a murderer."

"But she didn't turn them in or tell anybody?"

"He was still her nephew, and Missouri is a capital punishment state. She probably didn't want him to get the death penalty, at least not because of her"

"So what do you think she did?"

"I think she hid them again."

EIGHT

DEATH'S HUNCH HAD TO wait. For the rest of the week, Wren was busy with a heavy schedule of auctions. On Friday, the one day she finished early, it was Death who was gone. He left early in the morning, not saying where he was going, but promising to be back as soon as he could.

He returned just as the sun was going down. Wren had been catching up on housework and she paused in the act of cleaning the new glass in her front window to watch him climb down from his Jeep. He moved slowly and stiffly. Unaware of her scrutiny, his face was shadowed by pain and fatigue. A bead of window cleaner ran down, distorting his figure, and Wren quickly swiped it away and went to meet him at the door.

Seeing her, he put on a bright smile and injected a hint of a swagger in his step.

"Honey, I'm home," he called out, voice light with irony.

"Oh, good," she said, following him to the sofa and perching on the arm beside him. "I wish you'd speak to the Beaver. I think something happened at school today."

That earned her a genuine laugh.

"Now I feel under dressed," she continued. "When June Cleaver cleaned house, she always wore heels and a pearl choker."

"I don't know," Death said. He reached up to tug at a red curl that was escaping from the kerchief she'd tied over her hair. "I think you're rocking the Lucy Ricardo look."

She leaned away and laughed. "So, how was your day?" She was dying to know where he'd gone and what he'd done, but she wouldn't ask. If he wanted her to know, he'd tell her.

"Driving," he said. "Nothing but driving."

"Did you have to go very far?"

His green eyes took on a hint of mischief. "Actually, I just went across town, but I got stuck behind someone who drives like you do and it took me all day."

She swatted him with her dust rag and stuck out her tongue, then hopped up. "What would you like for dinner?" she asked, moving away. She was halfway to the kitchen when she realized he wasn't going to answer her. She turned back to find him staring at her seriously. "What?"

"You know, you don't have to feed me." There was something in his voice she couldn't readily identify. Pride? Embarrassment?

She shrugged. "You don't have to protect me from gun-wielding maniacs either. I was thinking lasagne."

He hesitated a moment; gave in. "Lasagne's good."

Twenty minutes later she was sliding the lasagne into the oven and wishing she'd baked bread earlier, when she had time. Death had gone into the back yard. She had a small vegetable plot there and he was picking the ingredients for a salad by the light of his flashlight. Wren hadn't heard a car pull up, so she jumped at the loud, imperious rapping on her front door.

She leaned into the living room with a certain level of trepidation, but the figure silhouetted against the street lights was small and feminine so she crossed the room and opened the door.

"Where's Death? I saw his Jeep out front."

The woman on the porch was small and dainty and stunningly beautiful. She looked like a starlet, fresh off the pages of a fashion magazine. Her dress was dark red, short and tight in all the right places. Her shoes, lips, nails, and handbag were all coordinated. She wore her dark hair in an elegant French knot at the back of her head and a filigreed gold locket on a delicate chain accentuated the curve of her bare neck and the perfect rise of her cleavage.

Wren stood next to her, in faded jeans and a ragged old tee shirt. She tucked an errant strand of hair back up under her kerchief and felt like a mutt at a dog show.

"Death's out back."

"Tell him Madeline's here."

Madeline. His ex-wife. Lovely.

Even as she bridled at the other woman's commanding tone, she forced her face into a pleasant smile.

"He'll be in in a minute." She stepped back and held the door wider. "Would you like to come in and wait?"

Madeline sighed deeply, as if horribly put upon, picked up an infant carrier that Wren hadn't noticed by her feet, and came inside. She stopped just inside the door and stood looking around.

"You can sit down if you like."

Madeline frowned suspiciously at the sofa and gave Wren a tight, insincere little smile. "I'll stand, thanks."

For two or three minutes the women stood there in an awkward silence. "So, I hear you cheated on your husband," seemed a poor conversation starter, and Wren suspected that whatever Madeline wasn't saying was just as bad. It was a relief to hear the back screen door slam.

Madeline set the infant carrier down and deftly removed the baby, pointing him at the doorway as Death's voice preceded him into the room.

"Wren? Did you know the handle on this bucket is cracked? You need to be careful not to pinch your fingers. Hey! Do you know I picked three different tomatoes and something had taken a single bite out of the bottom of each one. I think maybe you got a tiny little Goldilocks infestation."

He came through the door into the living room and stopped.

"Madeline."

Madeline waved the baby's fist at him and gave him a smile that was a lot brighter than the one she'd given Wren, though to Wren's discerning eye it still looked phony. "Look who wanted to come spend some time with the big guy!"

Death's face hardened. He crossed the room in quick strides and took the baby, tucking him up against his left shoulder. "No," he said shortly. He picked up the infant carrier and thrust it into Madeline's arms, slipped his gun out of the back of his waistband and herded her, protesting, toward the door.

"Death! What the hell?"

He backed Madeline up against the door frame, opened the door and peered at the yard suspiciously for several seconds. Then he pushed her through. "S'cuse us," he said over his shoulder to Wren, before following Madeline outside.

Wren stood for a minute staring at the closed door. *Well,* she thought, *that went well.* Eaten up with curiosity but too proud to eavesdrop, she hesitated for a moment. She had an urge to pull off her kerchief and go for a comb, but there was nothing she could do with her hair that would ever let her compete with someone like Madeline in the beauty department.

Not that she was, of course. Competing, or anything. She and Death were just acquaintances, friends. Cohorts, maybe. And there was nothing to suggest that he even thought of her that way. In fact, if Madeline was an example of what he looked for in a woman, then it was highly unlikely.

But she was the one who was feeding him tonight.

With a frustrated huff, she blew the loose curl off her forehead and headed for the kitchen to make a salad. *Turtles,* she thought, exasperated and amused. *A tiny little Goldilocks infestation indeed!*

———

Death backed Madeline up against the door frame and kept the baby carefully shielded between their bodies as he peered around the darkened yard. In times of deep exhaustion or high stress, he still sometimes saw the shadowy figures of armed insurgents flickering among the trees and cars at the corners of his vision. The ghosts of snipers and suicide bombers had followed him home. He knew they were only hallucinations, but they were unsettling, especially when there was a very real gunman out there somewhere who might be targeting him.

"S'cuse us," he said over his shoulder to Wren, sparing a second to regret her having to see this freak show that was his failed marriage. He hustled Madeline out the door and toward her car.

"What the hell?" she said again, as he opened the back passenger door and motioned for her to strap in the baby's car seat.

"What the hell?" he echoed. "What the hell are you doing here? Don't you listen to the news? There was a man shooting at us less than a week ago." The baby curled Death's shirt into his tiny fist and nuzzled his shoulder. Death tightened his hold on him and scanned the shadows again, gun at the ready.

Madeline snorted. "That was almost a week ago. He's long gone."

"That doesn't mean he won't come back. You don't put your baby in the path of a gunman!"

She finished fixing the car seat and stood to study him critically. "You know, paranoia is one of the symptoms of PTSD."

"I don't have PTSD."

"Sure you don't."

She took Benji and put him in his carrier, and the loss of the baby's warmth left Death with a cold spot over his heart too sharp for the mild night to account for.

"Come on, sweetie. I thought Death might want to play with you for awhile, but I guess he doesn't love you after all."

Death grabbed her arm and growled at her, voice low and rough.

"Don't you do that Madeline! Don't you use your baby that way. It isn't fair. It isn't fair to him and it isn't fair to me."

"Life isn't fair," she shot back.

"That's just a cliché people use to justify doing something they know is wrong."

She jerked her arm away and slammed the car door. "You know what? I get that you're pissed at me. I do. But I tried, Death. I tried to take care of you. I tried to be there for you. I did my best."

"Really?" His voice rose half an octave in disbelief. "That's how you remember it? Really? Because the way I remember it, you wrote me a Dear John letter while I was in a coma. And knowing what was already waiting for me when I woke up."

"*If* you woke up. Some of the doctors didn't think you would."

"So that's your rationale? You figured it was okay to screw me over because I might not live to find out?"

"It wasn't like that. I just hit a wall. Everything that happened, I was the one who had to be strong. I'd been trying for years to hold you together. You're just too broken. There's not enough glue in the universe to put you back together. I realized that and I just couldn't do it anymore."

"You were all I had left and you abandoned me." The guy in the next bed over in Germany had a girlfriend who was afraid to fly. She spent sixteen hours on a plane to be with him. Everyone there had someone, in person or in spirit. Everyone got phone calls or letters or care packages. Everyone but Death.

"I came back," she said.

"Only because you needed something. You always come back when you need something."

"I'm here now."

"You have a date. You're looking for a babysitter. Do you think I don't know what it means when you dress that way?"

She had the grace to drop her eyes as she moved away and circled the car. She paused by the driver's door.

"It doesn't mean anything. It's just a guy I know from work. He asked me to dinner." Her voice turned plaintive. "I don't get to go out much anymore, Death. Money's been tight."

She looked at him expectantly, as if she thought he'd reach for his wallet to make it better. It wasn't an unreasonable assumption: for years he'd done just that. But times had changed. He'd changed.

He'd had no new paying jobs since he captured Tyrone Blount. That bounty was almost gone. It had taken more than half of what he had left to put gas in the Jeep for the long drive up to Columbia. He'd left the VA with his disability paperwork still caught in a bureaucratic backlog, a disappointing lack of progress in the condition of his lungs, and a prescription for pain pills he desperately needed and couldn't afford to actually buy.

He was facing the prospect of being destitute—again. Of skipped meals and hocking his belongings and collecting cans on the highway to buy gas. Only this time it would be worse, because there were people who had taken an interest in him and who would realize he was in dire straights. He thought of Chief Reynolds, of the Keystones and Wren Morgan.

These people had been kind to him. He did not want to be piteous in their eyes.

"You took almost everything I had," he told Madeline, his voice so defeated his soldiers would have never recognized it. "I gave you everything I had left. You can't keep asking for more."

"You could come home," she said softly.

He didn't look at her. "You know I don't have a home anymore."

"Just ..." she sighed and didn't finish the sentence. Presently he heard her car door close. The car engine purred quietly to life, and then she was gone.

———

When Death went back inside, the house smelled like tomatoes and garlic and oregano. He paused in the living room and put some classic rock on the stereo, hoping Credence and Kansas would drown out his stomach growling. He hadn't eaten anything but a bowl of cold cereal almost sixteen hours earlier. His mouth was watering and the cooking scents made him lightheaded.

The lasagne and salad were already on the table, sitting between two place settings of Wren's eclectic collection of mismatched Depression glass. She'd found the flowers he'd put on top of the vegetables in the plastic bucket. They were really only weeds, he supposed —black-eyed Susan and Queen Anne's lace—but Wren had arranged them in a blue glass vase in the center of the table, giving them pride of place as surely as if they were hothouse orchids from a pricey florist.

She was working on the cracked plastic handle that was supposed to protect one's hand from the metal bail on the bucket. Death leaned against the refrigerator and cocked an eyebrow at her.

"You're fixing it with duct tape?"

"Sure. Why not? You can fix anything with duct tape!"

"Anything? Really? Is it better than glue?"

"Yeah, maybe." She considered. "What did you have that needed fixing?"

He quirked one corner of his mouth up in a humorless smile. "Nothing important."

She gave him a puzzled frown but let it pass. "Come sit down," she said, putting away the bucket and the tape. "Dinner's about ready. There's garlic toast in the oven, but it should be done now."

He sat down and served out the lasagne and salad and she got the toast out of the oven and arranged it in a napkin-lined basket. She offered it to him as she took her seat.

"There aren't any auctions on the schedule for tomorrow. The Keystones have a family wedding to go to, so we can spend the whole day looking for the jewels if you want."

"You're pretty close to the Keystones. Don't you want to go to the wedding too?"

"I'd rather go treasure hunting with you."

Death smiled at her, warmed by her simple honesty. A little voice in his head was wondering if she'd want to spend time with him if there were no jewels involved. Rather than dwell on that, he toasted her with his coffee.

"Tomorrow, then."

She smiled and clinked her soda can against his cup.

"Tomorrow," she echoed.

NINE

"Catching anything?"

"Not yet."

"Maybe you're not using the right kind of bait."

"Maybe not. What do you suggest?"

Roy Keystone leaned out over the well housing to peer down the deep, dark hole. Death had removed the cover—a terra cotta disc the size of a dinner plate with holes in it to admit the pipes and wiring—and dropped a fishing line with a three-pronged hook on the end.

One of the older grandsons, a skinny boy in his late teens, piped up. "Tie my girlfriend to it and drop her down there. If there's any jewels, I guarantee she'll find them. I swear I can't go anywhere without that woman dragging me into a jewelry store."

"She wants you to buy her an engagement ring," Sam informed his grandson.

"Engagement ring!" the kid squawked. "I don't wanna marry her!"

"Then what are you dating her for?"

"I'm just ... you know ... test driving her. Didn't you ever test drive a car you didn't really want to buy?"

All the men gathered around watching Death's fishing expedition snickered but, he noted with amusement, they also all looked over their shoulders to see if any of the women were close.

"Kid," Death said, "do yourself a favor and don't ever say a thing like that where one of the ladies can hear you."

"I might want to marry her someday," he defended himself. "Maybe. It could happen. Probably not, but you never know, you know?"

"What do the women in the family think of her? Your mom and grandma and whatnot?"

"Aw, they don't like her very much. But that doesn't necessarily mean anything."

"No, maybe not, but it's something to think about. You know, the women in my family, my mom and grandma and great-grandma, they all hated my wife. They thought she'd take me for everything I owned and cheat on me the minute my back was turned."

Death sensed a sudden cooling in the atmosphere.

"You're married?" Roy asked.

"Not anymore."

"What happened?"

"She took me for everything I owned and cheated on me the minute my back was turned."

That drew a laugh, and for the first time since his divorce Death found himself laughing along, albeit ruefully.

"Hardly an auspicious topic of conversation," Sam noted, "today of all days."

"Oh, don't be a prude," Roy scolded.

The Keystones were all in their Sunday best, with the women in dresses and hats and heels and all the men except Roy in suits. Even he had foregone his usual overalls for slacks and a dress shirt with a tie.

"Besides," Roy continued, "everything worked out okay for Death. He's seeing Wren now, after all." He shot the younger man a sharp look. "You are seeing Wren, right?"

Death squirmed. "Not exactly seeing her, I don't think. We've been hanging out a lot. She's a nice girl."

"But?"

"Man, my life is so screwed up right now, I'm just not in a position to be courting a lady."

"Courting a lady?" Roy scoffed. "Listen to him, Sam! He sounds older than we are!"

"Screwed up how?" Sam asked.

"Oh, you know. I got kicked out of the Marines, don't really have a steady job. I'm living on what I can make as a bounty hunter, and let me tell you, it ain't much."

"Right, so first of all, you didn't get 'kicked out of the Marines.' You got a medical discharge, and a couple of medals from the way I hear it. And you should be getting disability. They're not screwing you around on that are they?"

"Not ... exactly. See, when I first got hurt I was reported KIA. I'm just having a little trouble convincing the paymaster that I'm not really dead. I should get something eventually, and that'll help a lot. Maybe then I'll be more set to chase girls."

"Ah, I see," Sam said. "So what you're saying is, you want to get your life in order, and then you'll be ready to ask someone to share it with you. Is that right?"

"Yes! Exactly!"

"Uh huh." Sam took off his ever-present fedora and smacked Death on the head with it, hard.

"Yowch! What was that for?"

"You've got it backwards. First you get the girl, then you build your life *together*."

Roy was cackling. "My brother: Dear Sammy. We've got to set this old man up with his own advice column! He's right though. If you like Wren and she likes you, don't go waiting around on account of pride. Even if it means letting her take care of you a little bit now, that's okay. Women love that sort of thing. Then later, when the situation's reversed, you can take care of her."

"I just don't want to be the kind of man who sponges off a woman."

"And I'm not saying you should be. Just that it's okay to lean on someone a little bit until you can get back on your feet." Roy looked him over, considering. "Just how messed up are your lungs, anyway?"

"Wren said he passed out on her the other day," the grandson who didn't want to be engaged offered. The other men all snickered and the kid turned red. "I don't mean he passed out *on* her, I just mean that he passed out ... on her."

"Though that is yet another area of concern," Death offered with wry humor.

"See, now? You can't be thinking that way," Roy scolded. "You'll just psych yourself out. Just figure on being creative. If you can't do pushups, you let her do pushups."

"Now, let me get this straight," Death said. "Are you guys playing matchmaker here? 'Cause I thought that was women's work."

"Well, *somebody's* gotta do it. You sure don't seem to be making any progress on your own."

"Maybe we're just old-fashioned. Nothing wrong with taking things slow, y'know."

"Oh, sure. You think that now. Young people always think they've got forever, but you're not gonna believe how fast old sneaks up on you. One morning you wake up and look in the mirror and it's like, 'whoa! I've got wrinkles? What happened to all my hair?'"

"Hsst!" one of the sons warned. "The women are coming!"

"Quick! Everybody look innocent!"

"Roy Keystone," Leona said, "you wouldn't look innocent with wings and a halo. Are you boys about ready to go?"

Death grinned at her and gave a silent sigh of relief.

"No," Roy said, surly like a little boy, "but somehow I don't think that's going to save us."

"You think right," his wife agreed. She turned to Death. "Are you finding anything?"

"No, not so far."

"Do you really think Mrs. Fairchild might've dropped the jewels in the well?"

Death shrugged. "It's the best way I can think of to keep them from ever being found, but I don't really know. I never met her, you know. What do you think?"

"I suppose she might have," Leona acknowledged. "I doubt it though. If she knew what they were she had to know how valuable they were, and I can't see her just pitching them down the well. Plus, I suspect there was at least a little part of her that thought they should be found and Declan should be punished. She just didn't want to be the instrument of that punishment."

"Are you going to stay out here when we're gone?"

Death heard the worry in Roy's voice and understood.

"No, I think maybe we'll give this up for now and go search inside some more. Probably better not to be out in the open with just the two of us here."

"Why's that?" the grandson asked.

"Missing jewels. Dead bodies. People shooting at them. Any of this ringing a bell?" Roy nudged Sam. "This kid one of yours or one of mine?"

"Damned if I know."

"You're both very funny," Leona said. "Now, everyone, if you will, please begin to make your way to the vehicles in an orderly manner. And I do remember Mary Beth's Christening and I *will* be doing a head count. I'm looking at you, Matthew."

"Gotta give the boy credit," Sam said. "That was one hell of a hiding place."

As the Keystones made their reluctant exit, Death reeled in his line one last time and went to stand with Wren, who watched from the verandah, waving goodbye.

"I know the Keystones are like family to you. I sure don't want to keep you from whatever wedding it is they're going to, if you want to go."

"Cousin Collette's wedding," she said, "and nobody *wants* to go, but I'm not really related by blood or marriage, so I have an out. Collette's a hag and her boyfriend—sorry, fiancé—is a weasel. They have this odd, dysfunctional relationship where they're either throwing things at each other, things like knives and bricks and hot skillets full of food, or they're telling everyone in great and unwanted detail about their sex lives. They're only getting married to have a big party and force their families to bring them things."

"Don't hold back, Wren. Tell me what you really think."

Wren made a face, smacked his arm, and went inside. Death followed her. "Wait up a second. I'm probably being paranoid, but I'd feel better if we went through the whole house to make sure we're alone, and check that all the windows and doors are secure."

They circled the ground floor first, making sure everything was locked up and secure. Death had to resist the urge to clear the place, room by room, as he would have searching for insurgents in Afghanistan.

"I feel like we should be kicking doors open and yelling 'clear,'" Wren said, and he wondered if she was reading his mind.

"You wouldn't want to be kicking this door down," he observed, checking out a dark pantry with a single, tiny window. "These shelves don't look too sturdy, hit them with the door and you'd wind up with—" he peered at the nearest label "— strawberry jam all over the floor."

"Oh! Mrs. Fairchild's strawberry jam! This was so good. She always brought it to bake sales and such. She loved to garden and make preserves, but she lived all alone and couldn't use very much. She gave a lot of fresh produce away all summer, but she also canned things all during the growing season, pickles and relishes and jams and jellies and canned fruits and vegetables. Then, every year at Christmas, she'd donate all of it to the Food Bank, to help feed the poor. There was even a bit in her will saying that anything left in her pantry was supposed to go to them, but Declan tied the estate up so long, they decided it probably wasn't safe to eat anymore."

"That's too bad. She sounds like a nice lady."

"I think she was. I didn't really know her very well."

"And it's especially a shame about the strawberry jam." Death looked down at Wren and allowed himself a tiny leer. "I can think of good uses for strawberry jam."

After checking the bedrooms on the second floor and the crowded attic, they wound up back in the parlor, or, as Wren had come to think of it, the Naked Dead Guy Room. Death took a second to replace the riser over the opening to the hidden compartment, then climbed the spiral stair with complete unconcern. Wren hovered near the bottom of the steps and tried not to touch anything that Naked Dead Guy might have come into contact with.

"You coming?" Death called over his shoulder. "The view from the cupola ought to be something."

"That's okay. I'll just stay down here and watch your backside."

He stopped.

"What?"

"Back. I'll stay down here and watch your back."

He grinned down at her. "Miss Morgan, I think your Freudian slip is showing."

She felt her face flame, but lifted her chin defiantly. "Maybe I just think your backside is worth watching."

He turned away and waggled his butt at her teasingly. She grinned at him, but then grew serious.

"Death?"

"Yeah?"

"Don't fall down the stairs and break your neck, okay?"

Glancing back, he winked at her reassuringly. "Don't worry. I have the grace of a cat."

"Uh huh. Thomas is about as graceful as a drunken hippo."

Death laughed softly, but made short work of lifting the trap door and checking the cupola for intruders. When he had closed and bolted the door again he came down the stairs with exaggerated care. "So, are you ready to find some jewels?"

"Where do you want to start?"

"How about right here?"

"In the Naked Dead Guy Room?" she asked in dismay.

"The parlor. It's called a 'parlor.'"

"Right. The Naked Dead Guy Parlor. Why do you want to start here?"

"It's an odd-shaped room. I thought there might be some kind of secret hiding place built into the walls or floor here."

"I thought you discounted secret hiding places."

"For the Civil War jewels. Because if they had been in one, Carolina's husband would have found them. But there could still *be* a secret hiding place. If there is, it stands to reason that Mrs. Fairchild would have known about it and that could be where she hid the jewel robbery jewels."

"Oh." She looked down. "That makes sense."

Death turned and gave her a penetrating look. "You don't have to stay in here with me if you don't want to," he told her kindly. "Just keep away from the windows and shout if you need anything."

She left him crawling across the parlor floor, rapping on the floorboards every few inches, and wandered around the hall. The open library door caught her attention and she drifted inside. It was more a library in name than in fact. The bookcases alone were probably worth more than everything she owned, but there were more books in her own collection. The massive desk sitting in front of the locked French doors was drool-worthy, though. She looked at it longingly, remembering Death's warning about avoiding windows. A French door, though, she reasoned, was not technically a window.

Plus, it was covered with a wooden blind, so it wasn't like anyone could see her through it.

She tiptoed over to the desk and gingerly settled herself in the plush, modern office chair behind it. "I am Ava Fairchild and I am going to hide these jewels," she told herself, trying to imagine herself in the older woman's shoes. "Where shall I put them to keep them safe?" She looked first around the room, then down at the desk itself. The desk top was four feet wide by seven feet long, fashioned from a single slab of walnut. It was as big as a coffin, she thought, and then tried not to wonder if it had ever been used to lay out the dead.

There were seven drawers, three down each side and one long, shallow one in the middle. Wren pulled them open one at a time, finding only a handful of random office supplies. She hadn't really expected to find the jewels just sitting in the desk drawer, but she knew enough about antique furniture to know there was a chance of a secret compartment.

She took the drawers out one by one, dumping each out and checking it for a false bottom, then laid them side by side along the top of the desk. The central drawer and five of the side drawers looked just as she would have expected, but the middle drawer on the right-hand side was a good six inches shorter than it should have been.

"Bingo," she said softly, and knelt to peer into the cavity where it had been. A solid sheet of wood blocked off the end. If she'd not known the drawer was too short, it would have looked just like the space behind any of the other drawers. She reached in, barely able to touch it with the tips of her fingers, and tried prying it outwards with her fingernails, pushing it to one side and then the other and flipping it both up and down, but nothing worked.

Frustrated but not discouraged, she pulled out the chair and got down on all fours to crawl into the knee-hole. In the dim light, the wood seemed smooth and unbroken. She slid her hands across the section that should cover the secret compartment and could feel a fine line around what had to be a door. She pushed and tugged to no avail, until she lost her temper and slapped her hand down just outside the edge of the cover.

There was a tiny *snick* as a catch disengaged and a three-inch-square door popped open in her face.

TEN

HOLDING HER BREATH, WREN reached into the secret compartment and was mildly disappointed when her hand only encountered a stack of brittle paper. She pulled it out and felt around carefully to make sure there was nothing else in the hole, then she closed the little door and backed awkwardly out of the knee-hole.

Sitting back down at the desk, she returned all the drawers to their rightful places and dumped their contents back in haphazardly. Then she lay her find on the polished surface. It was a stack of paper, good quality but yellowed and obviously very old, tied with a faded silk ribbon that had probably once been pink or red. With exaggerated care, she eased the knot loose and spread the stack in front of her. The stack was made up of smaller bundles, each five or six sheets thick and folded once in the center. Letters, she realized, smoothing the top one carefully.

My darling Eustacia,

Wren frowned, trying to match the name to a member of the Campbell family. When she came up blank she carefully lifted the top sheets to peer at the bottom of the last page:

Thy doting husband, Obadiah

Obadiah. Obadiah Healy, of course. Wren shifted in her seat and tried to swallow her rising excitement. They might not be jewels, but two-hundred-year-old love letters from the famous artist could have real historical value. Turning back to the top sheet, she began to read.

My darling Eustacia,
I am sitting alone here in my room at the inn, watching a pink dogwood bloom outside the window and missing thee, as I ever do when sorry circumstances force us apart.

("Aw," Wren murmured.)

I have been touring the site of our new capitol and visiting with some of the statesmen who will be living and working here. It is an exciting time to be an American, watching the architects of buildings and the architects of nations as they labor together to take us forward into this new century.

("Oh, wow!," she whispered.)

Everyone is very optimistic for the future, in spite of the continuing difficulties with England. There is to be a national gallery, eventually, and I have been commissioned to provide several portraits for it, and also a number of landscapes show-ing Washington, D.C. before and after construction. I have also been invited to contribute my little pen-and-ink drawings to the newspaper that is to be established. I spoke with Mr. Mon-roe this morning and he was, in particular, very complimentary about Gentlemen Dancing.

("Eh?")

So, Dear Eustacia, all in all it has been a very profitable trip. I am increasingly anxious for it to be over, though, so that I might return to thine arms and to thy bed. For every night, and every spare moment during my waking hour, my thoughts re-turn to the sweet, sweet vision of thee, lying naked before me, and my loins burn with the desire to feel thee once more writh-ing in ecstasy beneath me.

("Oh, my!")

Three days! Three days hence, my love, and I will be once more by thy side. If thou hast guests, pray send them away. Banish the servants and draw the drapes and wait for me on the stairs in thy best red gown. For I would sweep thee up and carry thee at once to our bedchamber. Or draw thee into the parlor and lay thee down before the fire. Or strip the silk from thy quivering flesh and take thee right there in the doorway, ripping the buttons loose with my teeth, letting my tongue taste the sweet honey of thy skin as thou archest against me in thine own desperate need.

Death stuck his head in the door. "What's going on?"

Wren jumped. "Nothing!" It came out an octave too high. She cleared her throat and tried again. "Nothing." Too low. "Nothing at all."

"Huh. Three nothings. That's gotta be something." He wandered over behind her to look over her shoulder. "What are you reading?"

She slapped her hand flat over the old paper. "Nothing. Nothing. Letters. Old letters. Really old letters. They were in a drawer"

"Really?" He considered her, amused. "Really old letters about what?"

"Oh, you know." She knew she was babbling, but she couldn't stop. "Dogwood, Washington, paintings, Britain. Things."

"Uh huh." He leaned in close, oh *so* close over her left shoulder, reached both arms around her, took her hands and pulled them back against her body, holding her close as he read aloud.

"And I would bind thine eyes, that thee may not see from whence comest thy next pleasure. Mayhap, my teeth will nip and tease the hard buds of thy full nipples, mine hands caress the peak of thy desire or mine eager mouth descend into the hot, moist valley of thy womanhood.

"Whoa! You're reading porn?"

"It's not porn!" Wren protested.

"What do you call it then?"

"It's erotica."

"And what, exactly, is erotica?"

She sighed. "Classy porn."

"Mmm. Who wrote this?"

"Obadiah Healey."

"Should I know who that is?"

"I mentioned him, I think. Famous artist? He was Andrew Campbell's maternal grandfather. There's a lot of his work hanging on the walls around here."

Death nodded, then let go of one of her hands to reach down and turn to the next sheet. Wren yelped and clapped her free hand over her eyes.

"Oh, good Lord! It's illustrated!"

Death's face was brushing against hers and she could feel the muscles twitch in his jaw as he smiled "Go, Grandpa!"

It's art, she told herself, and allowed herself to peek.

The drawing took up the entire sheet. It was a woman lying on what seemed to be a bed of ripped clothing, naked but for an elaborate serpentine necklace. She was blindfolded, but otherwise unfettered. She lay on her back with her legs spread. Her left hand cupped her left breast and her right was stretched down to toy with her (Wren blushed) her *self*. Her head was tipped back, her mouth slightly open and the tip of her tongue visible.

"Hell of an artist," Death said, his voice husky. He reached out and ran one finger lightly over the drawing and Wren felt her own body responding as if he were touching her. She swallowed hard and moaned ever so slightly.

Death turned to the next sheet. There was another drawing, half the page this time, and more description.

Two naked bodies intertwined. "That's not even possible," Wren objected.

"Sure it is," Death countered, his voice low with desire. "It starts with a kiss."

She looked up to find him looking down at her, his expressive green eyes searching her face. His lips were less than an inch from hers. She had been wanting to kiss those lips since she first laid eyes on him. She rose up to meet him, wrapping one arm around his neck to hold him close as she finally let her mouth explore the contours of his. He kissed her back, greedy. Hungry. She let him draw her up out of the chair and lower them both, so that they wound up kneeling, facing one another.

Keeping one arm locked around his neck, she let the other slip under his tee shirt, exploring his smooth, strong back. She brought her hand around to the front and ran it up his chest, pausing as she encountered scar tissue. He stilled and caught her hand through the soft cotton.

Looking into his eyes, she read embarrassment and humiliation.

"Does it hurt?" she asked.

"No."

"Then it's okay. You've got nothing to be ashamed of." She kissed the corner of his mouth, his jaw and his collar bone and then tugged the shirt up so she could lean in and place a kiss above his heart.

"Turnabout is fair play, you know," he said, and slid both hands inside her own shirt. He let his thumbs ghost over her nipples, brushing the soft fabric of her bra against the tender flesh and making her writhe.

She wrapped both arms around his waist, pulling him as close as she could while his hands found her bra clasp and unfastened it. He reached into her sleeves, one by one, and drew her bra straps down off her shoulders. When they were free, he pushed her away just enough to allow him to reach up between them and pull the garment loose.

At the small of his back she encountered the metal of his gun, warm from being in contact with his skin. *I'm making out with an armed man,* she thought. She pulled it out and set it on the chair seat, then took advantage of the gap it left to slip her fingers inside his waistband.

In a swift move, and one she wasn't expecting, Death flipped her tee shirt up and leaned down to suckle her left breast. She gasped, shuddering with desire, and pleasure shot through her like electric shocks. She tipped her head back, half closing her eyes in ecstasy, barely registering anything in the world except for the man in her arms. But then something, some sixth sense, warned her that something wasn't right.

She blinked the room into focus, stiffened suddenly, pushed Death away and screamed like a banshee. Dark, lustful eyes set in a pallid face watched them from just beyond the desk.

Declan Fairchild was standing in the room with them, watching them make love.

———

"Tell me what happened."

Chief Reynolds watched as Death paced the library nervously, peering out the open French window, drumming his fingers against his thigh.

"Wren Morgan and I were at the desk, reading over some papers she found."

"That shade of pink looks good on you," the chief interrupted

Death blinked. "What?"

"Pink." The chief pulled a clean handkerchief from his breast pocket and wiped Death's mouth with it, like the ex-Marine was a school child. He held it up to display a pink smear.

Death blushed. "We were reading some papers she found. And she might have kissed me."

The Chief refolded the handkerchief to another clean spot and wiped it over Death's cheek and jaw.

"...a couple of times..."

He re-folded it again, spat on it, then tugged the neck of Death's tee shirt down and scrubbed at his collar bone.

Death sighed and hung his head.

"We were making out on the floor behind the desk," he said.

"There, now. Was that so hard? And...?"

"And all of a sudden Wren starts screaming, and not in a good way, if you know what I mean. I look up, and Fairchild is standing there watching us. Freaking pervert! I grabbed for my gun."

"Where was it?"

"Right next to us, on the chair seat. Anyway, I grabbed it and tried to jump up, but I was short of breath and when I got up I got light-headed. Gave Fairchild time to get out the French window and across the porch. I went after him, but he had a motorcycle parked in the front yard and he took off. I didn't shoot at him because I was still dizzy and I wasn't sure of my aim. There's a park on the other side of that fence and I didn't want to risk hitting an innocent bystander."

"Good call."

"What I want to know is, how did the nasty little pervert get in here? We searched the whole place and made sure all the doors and windows were secured before we started looking for the jewels. And we *were* looking for the jewels. Originally. And after I called you, we went through the house again and all the windows and doors are still locked from the inside."

"It was his aunt's house. He has a set of keys."

"The Historical Society had all the locks changed after he got in looking for the jewels last Sunday. Even if he has keys, they shouldn't open anything now."

"What about the oriel window with the broken lock? The one Whitaker got in?"

"Yeah, but Whitaker was a really little twerp. Even greased up and naked, Fairchild's not gonna fit through there."

"Well, then, he must have been hiding somewhere inside and you just overlooked him, don't you think?"

"Yeah, maybe. But then where did he get the motorcycle? It sure wasn't there when we came in the house." Death gave the chief a sharp look. "I've wondered if he might be working with someone. We know someone killed the jeweler before Fairchild broke out of prison, and we know that that someone was probably one of Ava Fairchild's shirttail relatives."

"Do we?"

Death frowned. "Don't we?"

"I expect we're probably on the same page here, but tell me your reasoning."

Death took a second to collect his thoughts. "Ms. Weeks said Halftree called her and wanted to talk about handling the sale of jewelry from Mrs. Fairchild's estate. She told him there wasn't any and he insisted he'd seen it. She suggested the jewelry was given or bequeathed separately to one of Mrs. Fairchild's friends or relatives. Friends can be hard to track down, but her obituary listed five surviving cousins and mentioned about a dozen more second-and third-cousins. I figure Halftree started calling them, looking for the jewels, and someone decided he knew too much and had to be silenced."

Reynolds sighed and shook his head ruefully. "I wish I could put you on my force," he said.

Death half smiled. "I wish you could too. You know, I come from a family of cops and firefighters. I always figured, if the Marines didn't pan out, I'd wind up being one or the other. My stupid lungs wiped out all three career choices in a single blow."

The chief slapped him on the shoulder encouragingly. "Yeah, well, just hang in there. I've got a feeling you'll do just fine as a private eye. Only..."

"Only?"

"Only, next time you start 'reading papers' with a pretty girl, pace yourself."

———

Wren perched on a stool in the Campbell house kitchen, leaning against the massive stone sink, seething with fury.

"I swear! The next time I see that horrible, nasty, creepy little pervert, so help me, God! I'm going to atlatl him just on principle!"

Officer Grigsby, standing by the back door, shook his head. "Listen, I understand you're upset, but you just can't be going out and hurting Eric Farrington. There's a waiting list for that."

She frowned at him. "I'm talking about Declan Fairchild."

"Oh, right. Sorry. It's just that you described Eric Farrington so well."

Wren laughed in spite of herself, then turned to the doorway as Death and Chief Reynolds came in. "What now?" she asked.

The chief shrugged. "We've updated the BOLO on him. Uh, that's a 'be on the look out.'"

"Yeah, I've seen that on TV."

"Right. We're trying to make the public aware that he's a wanted man. It's going to get real hot for him, real soon. For the time being, we'll have a patrol car driving by once or twice an hour. We're keeping an eye on your house, too, Wren. Just keep your eyes open, stay aware of your surroundings, and call us if you think you spot anything." He looked between them. "Are you going to stay here, or do you want to leave now?"

Wren and Death glanced at one another. "Do you want to leave?" Death asked. She could tell that he did not.

"You'd like to stay."

"I'd really like to see if I can figure out how Fairchild got in here. If he was hiding when we searched, then someone had to have brought him that motorcycle. But if you were working with someone and they needed a ride, would you lug a motorcycle around to leave it for them, or would you just wait for them in a car?"

"You think there's a hidden entrance?"

"I think it's possible."

"I don't mind staying," she said, "except that I'm starving. Do you really think that jam's no good?"

He gave her a sad grin. "Mrs. Fairchild's been dead for just over four years so, yeah, I'm pretty sure it's past its 'best by' date."

"Well, then, let me call and order a pizza and I'm good for the afternoon."

———

An hour and a half later, as they sat over the remains of a large, hand-tossed pizza and a collection of empty soda cans, Death gave Wren a sly, speculative look.

"I don't suppose you want to pick up where we left off when we were so rudely interrupted?"

She blushed furiously and hid her face. "I, um, usually, you know, I, um, I don't … rushing into things and all, you know. I … I just don't want you to think I'm a slut."

He laughed at that. "Do you think I'm a slut?"

"What? No! Of course not!"

"Good, 'cause I don't usually go rushing into things like that either. So, um, blame it on Grandpa Healey?"

"Blame it on Grandpa Healey," she agreed.

"Powerful artist," Death said.

"Powerful artist!"

They laughed together, giggly and relieved. Death wrapped his hand around hers and she squeezed his fingers and leaned against him, her heart light in her chest.

Then Death sighed and shook his head. "Man, I *know* Fairchild wasn't in here when we searched the place. I was a Marine, dammit. I know how to clear a house."

"Right. I agree. But how did he get in, then?"

"We checked all the windows and all the doors." Death was thinking aloud. "The doors were all locked and bolted with no sign they'd been jimmied. Some of the windows have locks that can be opened from outside with a pocket knife, but that would leave marks in the paint and there are none. The trap door from the cupola was bolted, the attic windows are painted shut. Are you sure there's no basement?"

"I've never seen any sign of a basement. There's a storm cellar that doubles as a root cellar out back, but it doesn't connect to the house."

"What about secret passages? This house dates to before the Civil War. Could it have been part of the Underground Railroad?" Wren was shaking her head before he even finished speaking. "Why not?"

"They came here from the South. They were slaveholders and Confederate sympathizers. Andrew fought for the Confederacy. Modern historians, especially ones with romantic notions about the South, like to claim that there were a myriad of socio-economic causes for the Civil War. And it's true that there were other contributing factors, but the central issue, the big reason for the whole she-bang, was the right to own slaves. Even Jefferson Davis, the president of the CSA, said that at the time."

"Yeah, I know. It's just …" He sighed.

Wren smiled sympathetically. "It's just that you're walking around their house, reading their love letters, hearing their stories, and you want to like them. But you keep getting hung up on the fact that they were involved in something reprehensible. I went to a thing the Historical Society put on once, a panel discussion about the Civil War on the border. Mrs. Fairchild was one of the panel members. She said it was important to never sanitize history, because we can learn much more from what we did wrong than from what we did right.

"She was always troubled that her ancestors had owned slaves. She said she felt she needed to do penance for them, so she always supported Civil Rights legislation, donated to the United Negro College Fund. I remember, just before she died, she organized an email protest when one of the big publishers put out a children's book about a black heroine with a picture of a white girl on the cover."

"She sounds cool, anyway."

"Yeah. And, you know," Wren's eyes went distant; she was lost in thought. "I think maybe she was superstitious, too. She said something about how her family had built their fortune on the back of an evil institution, which is why, she thought, that they'd never had any luck with the things that truly matter."

"What did she mean by that, do you think?"

Wren shrugged. "Carolina died in childbirth. Or shortly after and because of childbirth. Her son had three children, but only one lived to adulthood. His only son died in the trenches in World War One, leaving a young widow and two small children. One of them was crippled with polio. Eva and her husband lost their only child."

"I didn't know they'd had a child."

"A little girl. She drowned at a church picnic when she was ten. And then Eva's husband died when he was only in his forties."

"No wonder the poor woman thought they were cursed."

"Yeah. She said something like 'justice is implacable and blood will always, always out,' and she just hoped she wasn't alive to see the next round of vengeance." Wren looked up suddenly, meeting Death's eyes, her own alight with sudden understanding. "She wouldn't have dropped those jewels down the well, Death. And, wherever she hid them, she meant for them to be found when she was dead."

ELEVEN

"Now, if you'll look to my left and about halfway down the table, you'll see Jake holding up our next item: a shiny, green tricycle. Actually, this was supposed to come later in the auction, but we moved it up so that Roy and Sam would stop arguing about who got to ride it next."

The light weekday crowd laughed obligingly. *An auctioneer,* Wren thought, not for the first time, *was as much entertainer as merchant.* She sold the tricycle, half a dozen dolls, a roomful of nursery furniture, and a box of books before directing the crowd to the lawn and garden equipment in the side yard and handing the microphone over to Roy.

The cash table was set up inside the empty house this time. As she went inside to get a soda, she found Leona and Doris in the middle of a lull. Naturally, they wanted to talk.

"So, what exactly, were you doing while Declan Fairchild was sneaking up on you?"

Wren felt herself blushing furiously. "Nothing."

"Really?" The two older women exchanged knowing smiles.

Doris was the more demure one, so it was a bit of a surprise when she was the one who asked, "So just how naked were you when you noticed him?"

"I wasn't naked!" Wren yelped in protest.

They just looked at her, skepticism writ plainly on their faces.

"I was only topless," she admitted finally.

"Oh, honey," Leona said, "tell me that after you kicked Fairchild out, you went back and finished jumping that boy's bones?"

Wren sighed. "The whole murderous, creepy, peeping Tom thing kind of killed the mood," she admitted.

"What about last night?"

"Last night, Death slept on my couch. I think he was embarrassed that he got light-headed from making out. But, you know, I was pretty light-headed too, and I don't even have a war wound to blame it on."

The older women laughed.

"Give him time," Doris advised. She sighed. "My, Leona. Wouldn't you love to be young and in love again?"

"I'd certainly love to have the energy again. Don't really feel I have anything to complain about though. I've got my man, and we earned our gray hair and wrinkles." She turned to Wren. "And you didn't ever figure out how Fairchild got back in the house?"

"Not a clue. We're pretty sure he didn't come in any of the windows or doors after we'd checked them the first time, and if he was hiding, we don't know where. Death's actually wanting to look for secret passages, but I told him things like that don't happen in the real world."

"Well, now, I wouldn't be too sure of that."

A customer came in to pay off their purchases, and the conversation was put on hold while the ladies tended to him. When he'd left with his receipt and an armload of, if Wren was honest about it, junk, she picked it up again.

"You think it's really possible? That there could be a secret passage?"

Leona shrugged. "I've been around a long time, sweetheart. I've done a lot of auctions and I've seen a lot of houses. Wouldn't be the strangest thing I've ever run across." She thought carefully before she spoke again. Wren could almost see her mind turning. "You know, the Campbell house dates back to the 1830s. We refer to it as 'Victorian', but the High Victorian period didn't even start until about 1867. More likely, it's a Tudor floor plan with early Victorian architectural details tacked on. Now, the Tudor period was a time of deep social unrest, and heavy religious persecution. It wasn't uncommon for Catholic families of that time to have secret chapels and priest holes built into their homes, so they could practice their faith without being found out and hide their clergymen from the priest hunters."

"But that doesn't mean they'd include them in a house built in America several hundred years later, even if it was built to a similar floor plan."

"No, but large homes built in the American Northeast during the seventeenth and eighteenth century also often had secret exits and hidden rooms, to protect the inhabitants from Indian attacks and give them an escape route if they were under siege. Eighteen-thirty isn't that far removed from those days, and this part of the country was the wild frontier back then. A wealthy family from back east could have very easily felt that they needed a bolt hole in case of attack by wild animals or savage Indians."

"You know, I never thought of that," Wren conceded. "But if there's a hidden exit or a secret hiding place, how do we find it?"

"Next time you go over there, take our youngest grandkids with you and let them play hide-and-seek. If there's a hiding place or a way out, they'll find it."

Wren laughed. "Sounds like a plan. So, can we borrow them tomorrow?"

"After school, sure." Leona peered out the window, studying the crowd gathered in the side yard. "So where is your handsome-yet-still-regrettably-dressed young gentleman today, anyway?"

"Up at Warrensburg. He said he had some business to take care of."

———

Maybeth Turner shivered and wrapped her arms around herself. The spring days had been warm, but the nights were still chilly. It was only early evening, and already the cold had begun to set in. She was not dressed for this. Her clothes were thin and revealing, tattered and, if she were honest with herself, none too clean.

Tucking her hands into her armpits, she leaned against the light pole and did her thirteen-year-old best to look alluring.

A gray Jeep Grand Cherokee pulled up next to her. The driver ducked his head to look at her through the side window and she felt her heart stutter and thud in her chest. The man was gorgeous—movie star handsome. No lonely college boy. Way beyond what she'd come to expect from this part of town.

Maybe he's Prince Charming, she thought. *Maybe he'll fall in love with me and want to get married and we'll go to his castle and live happily ever after. Maybe he'll let me stay all night. Maybe he'll give me something to eat.*

Prince Charming powered down the passenger window.

"Hey, sweetheart. You need a lift somewhere?"

"Yes! Please!"

She heard the lock *snick* and fumbled with the door. She couldn't get in fast enough. The Jeep was warm and she sank into the seat and let it surround her. He manipulated the controls on his own door, rolling her window back up. She heard the lock snap closed again and refused to let it bother her.

Prince Charming had beautiful green eyes. She thought they looked kind, though the older girls had warned her that a man's eyes could be deceiving.

"What's your name?" he asked.

She batted her eyelashes at him. "My friends call me Baby Cakes."

He raised one eyebrow. "Baby Cakes. Cute. So, Baby Cakes, you hungry?"

"A little," she admitted, trying to keep the eagerness from her voice.

He went through the first drive-through they came to and got her a cheeseburger, fries and a chocolate shake. He didn't order anything for himself and she took her food with shaking hands and dug right in, half afraid it was a cruel joke and he'd snatch it back away from her. He just drove along in silence while she ate. She couldn't remember the last time she'd had a real meal and she refused to wonder what she was going to have to do to pay for this largesse.

Her prince didn't speak again until she was finished with the food and slurping the last of the milkshake from the cardboard cup.

"So, Baby Cakes, where you staying?"

She gave him a hopeful smile. "Anywhere you want me to."

"Oh. That's nice. How about your home, though? You do *have* a home. Nice warm bedroom. Soft, safe bed. Clean clothes, a hot shower, a refrigerator full of food. A family waiting for you."

She swallowed the lump in her throat, fought back tears. "Family don't mean anything," she said. "Family ain't nothing but a bunch of people you're related to."

She glanced over at him and saw something in his eyes that was too old and too complex for her to identify.

"Is that really what you think?" he asked.

"It's what I know."

"Mm hmm." He sighed. "Sweetheart, pop open that glove box. There's a picture in there I'd like you to see."

Setting her shake down in the cup holder, she opened the glove box and removed a four-by-six picture in a wooden frame. It was a studio portrait, a group of smiling, well-dressed people. An ancient, wizened old woman sat in the front with the others arrayed behind her in a fan shape. There were two couples, one not quite elderly and one in early middle age, and a pair of tall, handsome young men in elegant uniforms, standing together with their shoulders touching.

She ran her fingers over the glass, quickly picking out Prince Charming in the fancier uniform, blue and white with shining buttons and stripes on his shoulder.

"Is this your family? They look nice."

"Yeah." His voice was tight and he swallowed hard before he went on. "This was taken not quite three years ago, in the summer. Just before my last deployment. Mom wanted a picture of her boys in their dress blues. I'd just gotten promoted to gunnery sergeant and it was my first chance to show off my new stripes."

He reached across and tapped the picture by the younger woman. "That's my mom. Adele. She was an English literature professor. That's how my brother and I got our names. I was named after a detective in an old mystery series. I always tell people it's a family name, but really it's not." He grinned briefly and she grinned back. "My brother's name was Baranduin, from Tolkien, but we called him Randy. He thought Brandy sounded like a girl's name, so nobody called him that but me.

"Dad was a retired cop. Thirty years on the force. Grandpa was a firefighter, which is why Randy became a firefighter too. Randy was also a paramedic. That's what that snake symbol on his uniform means. It's a caduceus. Grandma was a lawyer. She was a district attorney at a time when women DAs were rare, and believe me, you did *not* want to find yourself arguing against her.

"The old lady in the front was my Nonna Rogers. She was my mother's grandmother. Great lady. She'd just turned ninety-seven, and she knew more about what was going on in the world than anyone I've ever met. And gossip! That woman loved her gossip. She was stone deaf, but it didn't faze her. She just learned to read lips."

"They sound nice," Maybeth said again, not really knowing what else to say.

"Yeah." He took a deep breath and when he spoke again his voice was tight. "You can't tell it from the picture, but my grandma Bogart was fighting breast cancer. She lost the fight a couple months later. After that, Grandpa pretty much gave up. He died within six weeks of her. The doctors said it was a stroke, but I always figured it was a broken heart. They'd been together since grade school and he'd never loved anyone else."

His eyes were dry, though his voice was pained, but Maybeth was quietly crying.

"Nonna died peacefully in her sleep just a little while after that. My parents were down because of all the deaths in the family, and lonely with me and Randy both out of the house, so they decided to get away for a bit. Go to the East Coast and watch the leaves change."

Maybeth looked over at him, fearful of what he was going to say next, and there were tears now rolling down his sculpted cheeks.

"They were killed in an accident on the Storm King Highway."

"Oh, God! That's so sad," she said. "So there's only you and your brother now?"

"No. Nine months ago I was wounded in Afghanistan. I was missing and presumed dead for a while and when I got back to our own troops, I was out of it. When I finally woke up, there was a chaplain there to see me. He'd come to tell me my brother had died in a fire." He pulled off to the side of the road, put the Jeep in park and turned to look at her.

"That picture was taken less than three years ago, and of all those people I loved, I'm the only one who's left. So don't ever tell me that family doesn't mean anything, Maybeth."

"I'm sorry," she sobbed. "I'm sorry! I didn't know. I just—" She froze. "How did you know my name?"

He pulled out his wallet and produced a laminated card.

"My name is Death Bogart. I'm a private investigator. I know your name because your parents hired me to find you. They're worried about you. They love you and they miss you and they want you to come home."

"They want me to?" she asked. "They really *want* me to?"

"You didn't think they'd want you to come home?" he asked, his voice rich with compassion and a touch of humor.

"I figured they'd be glad I was gone."

He gave her a sad smile, traded his wallet for his phone and called a number on speed dial. "Mrs. Turner? This is Death Bogart. I have someone here who wants to talk to you."

She took the phone like it was going to bite her, looked at it for a long minute, then put it up to her ear. "Momma...?"

———

When Death pulled into Wren's driveway, she was waiting for him at the door, her left hand cupped and tears in her eyes. He stopped a moment to speak with Tom Keystone, who'd been standing guard duty in front of the house, then came up the steps. He took one look at her and stopped.

"What's wrong?"

She held up her hand, displaying the contents. "My thing died."

"Oh. I'm so sorry." He looked down into her palm, bewildered. "Um, what was it?"

"You know, I don't know." She looked down too. The little creature in her hand was about the size of a peanut, almost embryonic, pinkish-white, with tiny legs and translucent little ears. "I found it in the yard at the house where we had an auction today. It was alive then and I thought that maybe I could save it and it would make a really cool pet . . . whatever. And when it grew up, I'd know what it was."

"I see."

She glanced up at him. "You think I'm nuts."

"I think you have a kind heart. That's never a bad thing. Listen, I need to ask you for a couple of favors."

"Of course. Anything."

He grinned briefly. "I've got a little girl, well, a young teenager, out in my Jeep. She's a runaway I was hired to find. Her parents are flying in from Denver and I need to take her up to the airport to meet them, but she's pretty raggedy and she doesn't want them to see her like that. Can she clean up here? And I thought maybe, if you still have some of your yard sale clothes, you could find her something less . . . slutty?"

"Yes, of course. That's no trouble at all."

"And then, I was hoping you'd come up to the airport with us. I'd feel better driving around with a strange teenage girl if there was another woman along. And this is the first actual case I've ever had and I thought, after I hand her over to her parents, we could do something to celebrate."

"I'd love to." She gave him a teary grin. "Did you have anything in particular in mind?"

"Oh, I don't know. Maybe one or two things." He grinned back. "I'll go get Maybeth and send her in. Why don't you give me your, um, thing, and I'll give it a nice burial."

She dropped the little body into his palm and kissed him on the cheek. He went back out to talk to the girl in the Jeep and in a moment Wren was welcoming her into her home.

While they were sorting through bags of clothing, finding her something nicer to wear, Maybeth looked up shyly. "Mr. Bogart's really nice. Is he your boyfriend?"

"Um, well, sort of. I'm working on it."

The girl smiled, but then her smile faded and she sniffled. "Was all that true? What he told me about his family? It's just so sad?"

"Why is that, sweetheart? What did he tell you?"

———

It only took Death a minute to dig a big enough hole to bury the dead whatsit. He shook his head, rueful, and tried to think if he'd ever known another girl who'd even pick up something like this, let alone cry when she was unable to save it.

Well, his mom might have. She'd have named it Wooster, or maybe Gatsby, and his dad would have shook his head and comforted her and taken care of the body, just as he was doing.

He'd been thinking about his family a lot today. He remembered now how much they had hated Madeline and wished, not for the first time, that he could introduce them to Wren.

He patted Lucy, who'd crawled out from under the porch to limp along in his wake, returned the shovel to the ramshackle shed where he'd found it and went back in the house, only to find himself with an armload of tearful redhead.

"Oh, Death! I'm so sorry! Oh, God, I'm so sorry!"

"It's okay," he told her, bewildered. "It was only a little hole. It was no trouble."

"I mean about your family. Maybeth told me what you told her. In the last three years, you lost your whole family. And you got injured and your marriage broke up and everything! My God! How do you go on?"

He tipped her head back and used his thumbs to dry her eyes. "I'm a Marine," he said gently. "That's what we do."

She buried her face in his shoulder again. "I just wish there was something I could say or do."

"Well," he suggested lightly, "there's always pity sex."

That made her pull back and peer up at him with a slight frown. "You can make jokes?"

"You can't cry forever, Wren. Sooner or later you have to find something to laugh about. Crying doesn't do anything but make your nose run." She held him close again and snuffled and he jogged her shoulder, teasing. "Are you getting snot on my shirt?"

"No," she said. "Maybe." She leaned back and gave him a calculating look. "Maybe you should take it off," she suggested, voice sultry.

The sound of a shower, which had been running in the background, cut out. Turning together, they both glanced at the bathroom door

"Or maybe not," Wren conceded with a sigh at this reminder they were not alone.

"That's okay," Death told her, brushing her hair away from her damp, flushed cheeks. "You can just undress me with your eyes until you get a chance to do it for real."

TWELVE

THEY HANDED MAYBETH OVER to her parents in a tearful scene at the airport. She and her mother were both crying and hugging everybody and her father couldn't stop shaking Death's hand.

"I can't believe you found her so fast," he said. He turned to Wren. "You know, we only called him this morning? Every other P.I. we talked to said it was almost impossible, and that, since they worked by the hour, they'd have to charge us more than we could afford. But then one of them gave us Bogart's name. He said he was just starting out and might be willing to work with us. And he was. He agreed to work for a flat rate, and not to charge us unless he found her, so of course, we gave him the job. But I never dreamed when I hung up the phone this morning that I'd be bringing my baby home tonight!"

He already had the check made out and as soon as Death wrote him out a receipt they took their leave.

"It's not going to be that simple, though, you know?" Wren said later, when they were sitting across from one another in a nice little Italian restaurant.

"What's that?" Death was concentrating on the breadsticks.

"The Turners. There have to be reasons why she ran away in the first place. Unless they address those, they're going to wind up right back where they started."

"Yeah, but now they know how serious she was about being unhappy and she knows how bad it sucks to be homeless, so maybe that'll give them the kick they need to get help." He took another breadstick from the basket, tore it in half and leaned across the table to feed it to her. "We can only do what we can do."

"You're awfully wise all of a sudden," she teased, when she could speak again. "Have you been reading more fortune cookies?"

"Maybe I'm just clever."

"Well, now, I suppose that's possible." She grinned. "So how *did* you find that girl so fast?"

He grinned and blushed. "Aw, it was nothing."

"No it wasn't. And you're dying to tell me."

"Well … yeah, actually, I am." He jumped up and gave her a peck on the cheek. "Wait here a minute. I gotta get my laptop."

He was back in just a couple of minutes with the oldest and most battered laptop computer she'd ever seen. He sat next to her this time, crowding her into the booth and sliding her plate aside so he could set the laptop where they both could see it.

She ran one finger across a gouge in the case "What happened to this thing?"

"Bullet," he said absently, opening it and flipping it on. He powered it up and called up a photograph. "Now, the Turners knew that Maybeth had been in the Kansas City area three weeks ago, because she posted to her Facebook page and the police were able to track the IP address of the computer she used to the Independence branch of the Kansas City Library. Police inquiries in Independence led nowhere and no one had any idea exactly where she was, until two days ago, when she texted a picture of herself to a friend, who posted it on *her* Facebook page. This is the picture."

Wren studied it. It showed Maybeth, dressed like a hooker, standing on a street corner. There was a post for a street sign, but the sign itself wasn't visible. In the background there was only the corner of a large building, made of faded red brick, a part of one curtained window visible. There was nothing identifiable that Wren could see. There was a fire hydrant, a cracked sidewalk, and a small section of cross street with one building visible. That was some kind of business, but any sign it might have had was out of the picture and its windows were obscured by a blue and white striped awning.

"Okay…?"

"So I found her from this picture," Death grinned, clearly pleased with himself.

"How?"

"Well, first of all, look at the building in the background. Not the one with the awning, the one right behind her. What do you see?"

"Um, bricks?"

"And?"

"Uh, part of a window."

"Good. And?"

"A curtain?"

"Right. And what kind of brick building has curtains in the window? Usually?"

Wren thought about it. "An apartment building?"

"Right! Now, this particular apartment building is pretty old. You can tell by how worn the bricks are. And it's not in a residential area. It's sitting right up against the sidewalk and that other building in the background is clearly some sort of business. Apartment complexes in small towns tend to be located in residential areas and they tend to be set back away from the road, with landscaping around them. So, it's not a guarantee, but I'm betting this is more likely to be either in the city or in one of the larger towns."

"Okay, but that still leaves a lot of room."

"Right. So, now look at the fire hydrant."

"It's a fire hydrant."

"Very good! Notice anything else?"

"… it's weird colors?" The fire hydrant was black and yellow with a green cap.

"Exactly! Now, I don't know if you know this or not, but there's actually a national color scheme for fire hydrants. The color of the cap signifies the available water flow rate. Most small towns can only supply less than 999 gallons per minute, so they get red or orange caps and usually they just paint the trunks red too and are done with it. This has a green cap, so it can deliver 1,000 to 1,499 gallons per minute. That suggests a city and goes along with what we've already figured out by looking at the buildings in the background. But then I ask myself, why a black and yellow trunk?"

"And did yourself answer you?"

"It did. See, myself knows, because my grandfather and brother were firefighters, that there are any number of reasons why fire hydrants get painted different colors. Some towns have their own color scheme, so do some neighborhoods. On Italian Hill, in St.

Louis, for example, the fire hydrants are painted the color of the Italian flag."

"Okay, but how were you supposed to find out who had yellow and black hydrants?"

"I'm a detective. I detected."

"Meaning?"

"One of the most common reasons fire hydrants get painted odd colors is because students from the local school paint them their school colors. I see black and yellow—black and gold—and I think Tigers. I tried Columbia first, because of the University of Missouri Tigers. They do have some black and gold hydrants, but they're painted in tiger stripes, not just plain colors. So then I started checking smaller cities. Sedalia and Warrensburg both have high schools with tigers for mascots. I started with Warrensburg, because it was closer, took this picture up and started showing it around the fire stations. Firefighters do maintenance on fire hydrants, so I figured if it was in their area, there was a good chance one of them would recognize it. One of them did. He gave me the exact address and then I just drove around until I found her."

Wren leaned in and kissed him on the cheek. "You know, you're really something. Pretty and smart too!"

He leaned his forehead against hers and sighed, oddly dejected in what should be a time of triumph. "Once upon a time I used to be strong, too."

She rubbed his back. "You're still strong."

"Not strong enough. I got light-headed just from kissing you. That's twice now I've let Declan Fairchild walk away."

"Okay, first of all, he didn't 'walk' away. He ran away like a scared little girl."

"You were throwing spears at him."

"It was just one spear, and that was just the first time. The second time he was definitely running from the wrath of you."

"Maybe." He sighed. "You know what happened to my family, Wren. I can't help but be a little bit paranoid. It really bothers me to think that I might not be able to protect you if you need it."

She had no answer to that and they sat for several long minutes in a companionable and not altogether happy silence.

"Teach me hand-to-hand combat!" she suggested suddenly.

"What?"

"Hand-to-hand combat. You're a Marine. You know that stuff, right? So teach me. Maybe you won't have to worry about protecting me so much if you know I know how to protect myself."

Death thought about it. "I suppose I could do that," he allowed. One corner of his mouth tipped up in a sly grin. "Do there have to be clothes involved?"

Wren grinned back. "Clothing," she assured him, "is entirely optional."

———

They were driving south, the hour getting late, classic rock playing softly on the radio, when Wren spoke suddenly.

"I don't want to go back to my house tonight."

Death looked over at her. All the dash lights were on his side of the car and he could only see her shadowy outline against the lighter darkness of the side window.

"Why not?"

"Declan Fairchild. He knows where I live. I'm so tired of being afraid of him. I just want one night, just to sleep without having to worry."

"I could take you to a hotel?" he offered.

"No," she said instantly. "I don't want to stay in a hotel. Could we go back to your place?" she asked, and his heart dropped, dread rising into his throat to choke him. "I could sleep on your couch. That'd be fine. You know, I don't even know where you live."

"Um, yeah, well … you know. That's kind of a problem."

Her head came up, he sensed more than saw her tipping her face in his direction. He could feel the puzzlement. She glanced into the back of the Jeep. It was too dark for her to see anything, but Death knew that she would have seen earlier what was back there, sleeping bag, air mattress, duffel bag of clothes, crate of food and toiletries. She had a sharp eye and a quick intellect. He waited for her to figure it out, for the disgust and condemnation. But, when she spoke, there was only warmth and concern in her tone.

"Death, have you been living in your car?"

"It's not a car, it's a Jeep," he deflected lightly.

"So that's a yes." She sounded like she was going to cry.

He reached over and found her hand, gave it a reassuring squeeze. "It's not so bad. Believe me, I've stayed a lot worse places." A cellar in Afghanistan came to mind, rasping for breath, his chest on fire, trying to keep Barlow from bleeding out and wondering how the hell they were ever going to find their way home.

"We can go to my house," she said. "It's okay."

"No," he shook his head. "No, I think you had a good idea. Hang on. I'm going to show you where I've been staying. Fairchild will never find us tonight."

They were still several miles out of East Bledsoe Ferry, on the west shore of Truman Lake, when Death flipped on his blinker and pulled off the highway onto a lane so overgrown it was practically invisible.

"What is this place?" Wren asked, speaking for the first time in minutes.

"Well, once upon a time this was a real road." The Jeep jounced and bounced along deep ruts. "Never a very good road," he admitted. "I drove it a few times with my grandpa, back when I was a little kid. It was a back road from Bristow to Grant's Crossing. It had the worst hill you've ever seen—practically vertical, with a long, narrow bridge at the bottom, over the Barker arm of Tebo Creek. It was a horrible bridge, one-lane and rusting out. I swear there were holes in the driving surface and you could see the water running underneath.

"Anyway, once the lake came in they took out the bridge and the water filled up that whole valley, so now this is just an old dead-end trail." He pulled to a stop at the brink of a hill, with trees thick around them, and the lake glinted briefly in the headlights before he switched them off and killed the engine. "Nobody comes here. It's not a good place to fish because it's too hard to get down to the water, and the road doesn't go anywhere. I like it though."

He got out and went around to open the door for her, then left her standing on the hill, looking out over the water below, while he got the air mattress and bedding out of the back.

He'd slept out under the stars here before, so there was already a place smoothed for the mattress, free of stones and other obstructions. He opened his sleeping bag and spread it on the mattress, then put a blanket over that, folding it back so it would be easy to slide under.

Wren was shivering slightly, rubbing her arms. "It is beautiful," she said, "but didn't you ever get cold?"

"Sometimes," he admitted, "but only because I was alone." He wrapped her in his arms and held her against him, then drew her toward the bed he'd prepared. "Come on, sweetheart. It's been a long day." They crawled under the covers and cuddled close under heavens that glistened with the light of a billion trillion stars. The ancient earth sang them the oldest love song of all, writ of crickets and tree frogs and night birds calling, of wind sighing in the leaves and water moving rhythmically against land in the darkness.

When Death awoke in the rosy dawn, Wren was curled warm beside him. Her head rested on his shoulder. Her red hair was splayed out across the pillow. Shafts of early morning sunlight lanced across the water, setting the whitecaps glittering and gilding the tops of the tallest trees.

For the first time in a long time, he felt like he was living in a state of grace.

THIRTEEN

"FORTY-EIGHT."

"Fo'ty-eight."

"Forty-nine."

"Fo'ty-nine."

"Fifty."

"Fiddy."

"Now what do you say?"

Bitty Sam, the smallest Keystone, tipped back his head and shouted at the top of his impressive lungs. "READY OR NOT, HERE I COME!"

The staircase in the main hall was base. He and Death had both been hiding their eyes against the newel post, a large golden head bent over a smaller one, while Death helped him count. The ex-Marine stepped back now and patted the four-year-old on the back as he launched himself off in search of his siblings and various degrees of cousins.

"Isn't it kind of mean," Death asked when the boy was out of sight, "making the littlest one be 'it'?"

"We'll help him if he needs it," Leona said, unconcerned. She and Wren were uncovering and cataloging the pictures and artwork on the walls. "Better than letting him hide. He's so little, last time he was missing for three days before we found him giggling in the bottom of the laundry hamper. Might still be missing if we hadn't had to do the wash."

"Really?" Death stared at her, aghast.

She gave him a long, level look. "No." She turned to Wren. "He's pretty, but he's gullible."

"It's a fair trade," Wren grinned. She uncovered another framed piece of artwork in the entry hall. "Oh, Death! Look. It's our favorite artist."

He crossed the room to peer over her shoulder. "I like his other artwork better. This is one of his political cartoons?"

"It must be. Something about Maryland. Not sure I understand it." It was a pen-and-ink drawing of a mighty tower. One of the foundations stones was emphasized and was clearly the outline of the state of Maryland. "Oh, I see. Sort of. The tower must be the United States and the foundation is a map of the original thirteen colonies."

"It probably made more sense at the time. Like I said, I like his other work better."

Wren smiled and blushed.

"So do I," Leona offered, voice wry. "So, by the way, does Mother Weeks. I really would avoid her if I were you," she told Death. "She gave poor Roy a finger hickey on his butt that will be sore for a month."

"You showed those letters to Mother Weeks?" Wren asked.

"I personally didn't. We decided to scan them into the computer so we could keep the originals in a controlled environment and still, ahem, study them. Somehow she got hold of a copy."

"There are copies?" Death asked, interested.

Leona grinned. "I'll get you a printout. Though I'd be very disappointed to think you needed help coming up with ideas in that department."

"Pretty sure he doesn't," Wren said, voice sly.

Leona raised her eyebrows. "A perfect man after all?"

"Well, we're getting there, I think."

Death, who had the feeling they were talking over his head and wasn't sure if he should like it, moved to the next frame, undid the straps holding the cover on and eased it loose. "This is another of his," he said.

"Well, he was an ancestor," Wren said. "It makes sense that they'd have lots of his artwork around the place." She came over to study the new picture. "Oh, this one I think I get. It's about the War of 1812. Or the buildup to war, probably."

The second cartoon showed a British naval vessel on the high seas, flying the Union Jack and with the officers and crew standing proud at attention in their fine uniforms, but the ship's reflection in the water showed the officers brandishing whips over a chained crew of bedraggled men in ragged, Revolutionary War–era American uniforms. The flag in the reflection was a tattered rendition of Old Glory.

"I think I remember something about that," Death said. "The British were boarding American ships and forcing the sailors to serve on British ships. British-born sailors, I think, and some Americans who had never been British got caught up in it. The Brits didn't recognize their citizens' right to emigrate and become nationalized

141

Americans, so when they needed sailors to fight their war with Napoleon, they took them off American merchant ships." He gave Wren a cheesy grin. "Do I get an A in history, Teach?"

Wren had moved on to the next picture. "I'll give you an A+ and a gold star if you can explain this one to me."

He went over and stood behind her, resting his chin on her head. "Buncha guys acting girly?" The third picture showed a tailor—obvious from the pins in his clothing and the tape measure around his neck—holding up an animal skin to a man dressed like Daniel Boone while a second frontiersman held another animal skin up in front of himself and admired himself in a mirror.

Wren shrugged. "I know men in the early nineteenth century wore elaborate clothes, usually. And trappers and explorers and whatnot didn't. So, I'd guess old Obadiah was making fun of somebody, though I couldn't tell you if it was the frontiersmen or the male fashion plates. I'll have to remember to ask Doris about it. She's our art expert. We're just uncovering these for her."

Death moved on. "This one's plain enough," he said. In the last picture on the east wall a group of men in fine suits and white wigs were milling around a conference table, lining up to sign some sort of document. Though the men were all smiling and shaking hands, they were also all holding knives behind their backs.

"That's plain?" Wren asked.

"Sure. It's politics. Two hundred years and it hasn't changed a bit. Well, except they have more teeth when they smile now and they've traded the knives for semi-automatics." He looked around. "Is it just me, or is it way too quiet in here considering the number of kids we turned loose?"

"It's not just you," Leona confirmed grimly. "If those little monsters aren't up to something, I'll eat my best hat."

Leona had brought over seven small Keystones, ranging in age from four-year-old Bitty Sam up to eleven-year-old Levi. Her instructions to them had been simple and straightforward: Stay on the ground floor; Stay out of the pantry, with its dangerously rickety shelves full of strawberry jam; Don't break anything.

Death found Bitty Sam in the bathroom, kneeling in the bathtub and peering up the faucet. "Anyone in there?" Death asked him.

"I can't see no one. It's awful dark, though."

"Yeah, I bet. Why don't we go look somewhere else?"

He tucked the toddler under his arm like a football and carried him out into the hallway, where they met Leona dragging nine-year-old Matthew along by one arm and scolding him furiously.

"I swear! You have as little sense as your grandfather! You've got that filthy stuff all over your clothes and you put your dirty feet on the racks—"

"Hey!" he protested indignantly. "You can't scold me for it gettin' me dirty *and* me gettin' it dirty. That ain't fair!"

"Isn't fair," she corrected. "And I can scold you for anything I want to scold you for. I'm the grandma. What would you have done if someone had turned it on, hmm?"

"Got out when it got hot?"

"Don't you sass me, boy!"

"You hid in the oven?" Death asked with a grin.

"It was a good place. Nobody found me."

"Gramma found you," Bitty Sam told him. "You 'it'!"

"She wasn't playing. That don't count."

They found Wren standing bewildered in the middle of the morning room. This room was lightly furnished with delicate furniture. The tall secretary was too narrow to hide even a child. The two sofas were too low for anyone to crawl underneath and the chairs and coffee table were too open. There were no closets or cupboards, only a bay window with a boxy window seat, the window covered with light, gauzy curtains.

"I could swear I heard children giggling in here!"

"Maybe it was ghosts," Matthew suggested. "You know this place is haunted. There's a lady in white and some dead kids and a Confederate soldier. And I bet that naked guy's here too, staggering around with his head on crooked."

Death smacked the boy lightly on the back of the head, like his father used to do to him and Randy. "Don't be so helpful." He crossed to the window seat, lifted the cushioned lid and peered inside, but the cavity below was empty. "Maybe they're in the parlor or the sitting room," he suggested. "This place has pretty screwy acoustics."

They went back into the hall and were halfway to the parlor when the door to the morning room burst open behind them and all five missing kids thundered out, stampeded across the hall and piled into the staircase, laughing hysterically.

"Okay," Death said. "Spill."

"It's magic!" Mercy Keystone was a rare girl in a boy-dominated family. She was a mixed-race child with coffee-colored skin and shining black curls and a beautiful smile. "D'ya wanna see?"

"Oh, absolutely."

They followed her back into the morning room and she lifted the lid of the window seat and climbed inside. "I'm gonna do a disappearing act. You gotta count to ten and say 'abracadabra' and then you can open the lid."

She curled up in the box and pulled the lid closed and Death turned to Wren. "Would you like to do the honors?"

With a smile, she obliged, counting slowly while muffled thumps and scraping noises came from the box and the other children hid grins behind their hands. "Abracadabra!" she finished.

Death was still holding Bitty Sam and he dangled him over the window seat. "Lift up the lid, buddy."

The toddler pulled the lid open and they all peered into the empty chest. Mercy popped up outside the window, pressed her nose against the glass and stuck out her tongue.

"Well," Leona said dryly, "I think we know now how Declan Fairchild got in."

———

"Bernie Kopek remembered the picture," Cameron said, passing over a five-by-seven color print of Ava Fairchild's obituary picture.

They were back at Wren's, sitting around the coffee table. Death had been picking flowers again and there was a big bowl of iris and daffodils and something spiky and blue-purple.

"Bernie's the staff photographer," Wren said.

"He said he took it at the Chamber of Commerce Christmas party, the week before Christmas. He remembered because Ava was all excited and she wanted him to be sure he got a good picture of her necklace. She told him that she expected to have exciting news soon, but the next time he saw her she was upset and told him to forget it. It had just been a mistake."

"When would that have been? Any idea?" Death asked.

Cameron shrugged. "Not too long. Winter is a slow news time, so we're always looking for stories. And Bernie's not known for being patient at the best of times. I know it was before Martin Luther King Jr.'s birthday. That's when Ava announced that she was leaving her house to the historical society."

"The third week of January," Death said. He lay the obituary photo beside his picture of the stolen necklace. Seen in color it was obvious the two pictures were of the same piece of jewelry. "So, at the end of December she finds the jewels hidden under the stair and thinks they're Carolina's jewels from the Civil War. She probably had just found them, within a day or two, before the Christmas thing. She wore one to the party and dropped hints, but she didn't want to announce that she'd found them until she'd had it confirmed. She went to Josiah Halftree, probably the week after Christmas."

"Why the week after Christmas?"

"She'd have wanted to go as soon as possible, but I can't see her taking a bunch of jewels out in public during such a busy shopping time as the last week before Christmas. I could be wrong, but that's my guess."

"Okay."

"Anyway, Halftree told her the jewels were too modern to be from the Civil War."

"But he didn't report to anyone that she'd brought them in," Wren objected. "Wouldn't jewelers have been sent descriptions of the stolen jewels and asked to look out for them?"

"Yeah, but remember, the robbery had been a couple of years before that, so it wouldn't have been fresh in his mind. And this wasn't just some random person bringing valuable jewels to him for appraisal. This was one of his oldest and most trusted clients. Probably she said she must have just forgotten buying them or something and he passed it off as senility setting in."

"Okay."

"Okay, so she finds out the jewels aren't the Civil War jewels and realizes that they must be from the robbery, which means that her closest living relative is a murderer. She changed her will on the fifteenth of January. I looked it up. Her health started going downhill after Christmas and in early March, she died."

"Did we tell you about the secret passage?" Wren asked Cam.

"This is off the record," Death interjected.

"You can't do that," Cam protested. "You have to say it's off the record before you say it. Once you say it, you can't go back and make it off the record. It doesn't work retroactively!"

Wren reached over, got Cameron by his immaculate tie, and pulled his face down until he was eyeball-to-eyeball with her. "It's off the record," she said.

"Yes, ma'am! Off the record. Absolutely! Anything you say!"

"We found a secret passage," Wren repeated. "Well, actually, the Keystone children found it. There's a window seat in the bay window in the morning room and one end opens to a short slide that lets out in the crawl space under the house. A sliding panel opens from there to under the verandah. Death booby-trapped it. Now the trap door only opens from under the house and the window seat lid only opens from inside the house. If Fairchild tries to get in that way again, he'll be stuck in the window seat until the police come to take him out."

Wren had supper cooking in the kitchen. There was bread in the oven, filling the house with its delicious, warm scent, an apple pie cooling on the windowsill and a pot of stew bubbling on the stove. She got up and excused herself to go check on it.

"Okay, question," Cam said.

"Shoot."

"If Declan Fairchild knew there was a secret entrance to the house, why did he send Flow Whitaker in the window, where he could fall down and break his neck?"

"Good question. I've been thinking about that myself and I've about concluded that he probably didn't. We've been assuming that Fairchild broke out of prison because he heard that Whitaker had been killed, but I talked to prison authorities. He actually escaped before the newspaper with the story of Whitaker's death was delivered to the prison library."

"So you think...?"

"Still off the record?"

"Sure."

"I think maybe Whitaker was working with whoever killed Josiah Halftree. We're guessing that was probably one of Ava Fairchild's cousins. Most people would have no idea how to go about selling stolen jewels. Declan Fairchild's cellmate could well be the only fence the killer had any knowledge of."

Wren appeared in the kitchen doorway. "If you guys want to eat, you'd better come and get it while it's hot."

Cameron stood and stretched, sighed regretfully. "I wish I could, sweetie. I remember how good your cooking is. I have to be at a town council meeting in a few minutes, though. There's a company trying to get a permit to put an adult bookstore in the old telephone company building, right downtown, on Main Street."

"That's a bad idea," Death said.

"You think so? Some people are saying it will bring in jobs. It's one of those big, warehouse-type businesses like you see on the highway."

"It'll bring in jobs until it goes bankrupt," Death shook his head. "Place like that, you need to hide it somewhere so people can sneak in without the whole town knowing what they're up to. Especially in a small town like this. I mean, hey. I kissed Wren at the donut shop this morning and fifteen people called her wanting the details."

"He knows," Wren said dryly. "He was one of them."

Cameron had the grace to blush. He turned for the door, but then turned back, hesitant.

"What?" Death asked.

Cameron cleared his throat. "I don't want you to think I was snooping or anything..."

"For wanting to know about a kiss?"

"No, not that." He shifted uncomfortably. He had picked up the folder he'd carried the obituary picture in and he fiddled with it and studied the floor. "I was ... curious about you. And I wanted to know what kind of man was hanging around Wren now. So I ... did a little research. I came across something. I don't know if you've seen this. Probably you have. But I thought, if you hadn't, or if you didn't have a copy, you might like to have it."

He handed over the folder.

Death looked at him for a long minute, then opened the folder while Wren hung back, studying his face.

"Oh, wow," he said. "I hadn't seen this. Wow. Thank you. Thanks a lot."

Cam half smiled. "It's no problem. I happen to know Wren has a huge collection of interesting frames, if you want to frame it. I'd bet she could find you one that fits it perfectly." He nodded to them both, then, and left, and Wren came over to lean against Death's arm and see what he was looking at.

It was a printout of the front page of the St. Louis newspaper. The feature story was headlined "FIRE SAFETY DAY AT RIDGE-WOOD ELEMENTARY" and a series of photos underneath showed schoolchildren climbing over a fire engine and listening, rapt, to a group of firefighters. One shot in particular showed a smiling young paramedic explaining something to a handful of kids.

"That's your brother?" Wren asked.

"That's Randy." He checked the date on the paper and swallowed hard. "Less than a week before he died."

"I'm so sorry! He was killed in a fire?"

"He died in a fire. The coroner said the actual cause of death was an aortic embolism. He must have had it all his life. Kid was basically a walking time bomb. I still can't believe we never knew. Firefighters have to be in really good physical condition, you know? They said it was just one of those freak things. But they said he went quick. He didn't suffer."

Wren traced her fingers lightly over the picture. "It says 'B. Bogart on his name tag. Shouldn't it be R. Bogart?"

Death grinned. "Our mother was an English Lit professor," he explained for the second time in three days. "Randy was short for Baranduin. It's from Tolkien. It was the proper Elven name of the river the hobbits called 'Brandywine.' Of course, I used to call him Brandy. He hated it."

"Brandy, you're a fine girl?" Wren guessed, singing softly.

"What a good wife you would be," Death agreed, not singing. He sighed. "I used to spend half my life coming up with new ways to torment my little brother. I wish he was still alive so I could do it some more."

FOURTEEN

"Ow! Ow! No! No! Stop! Don't do that!"

Wren turned loose and Death rolled away from her and tried to pretend he hadn't just been shrieking like a girl. He was dressed in loose gym shorts and a tee shirt and she was wearing a low-cut tank top and spandex tights.

"That's not nice," he scolded.

She grinned, crouched like she was getting ready to spring and flexed her hands like lobster claws.

"I'm only following advice," she said.

"Whose advice?"

"Mother Weeks, remember? Pinch butts now, while you're young, because no one will appreciate it when you're old."

"That wasn't my butt."

Her grin turned feral. "I know."

He leaned in and kissed her, using it as cover to reach around and pinch her butt. She shrieked and he backed away quickly, laughing. "Actually, you know what? That's a damn good move. Not to use on me!" he amended hastily, fending her off. "But if you ever get into a real fight with a guy, get hold of him like that and he'll be at your mercy."

There was a knock on the door and Chief Reynolds stuck his head through. "You two okay in here? Hope I'm not interrupting anything?"

They pulled themselves and one another up from the floor.

"Death's teaching me hand-to-hand combat," Wren explained.

The cop nodded. "Good idea, but you might want to go a little easier on her, son. I could hear her yelling clear down the street."

Death blushed and Wren snickered, but neither one of them corrected his assumption.

"Come on in," Wren invited. "Would you like some coffee?"

"Oh, I don't want to put you to any trouble."

"It's no trouble. It's already made." She went into the kitchen and returned with a cup of coffee for the chief. "I looked up 'care and feeding of a Marine' online and it said to always keep a steady supply of coffee handy."

Death went to the kitchen to refill his own coffee and brought Wren a cold bottle of strawberry soda and they all settled around the coffee table to talk. "Got any word on Fairchild?" Death asked.

The chief shrugged and shook his head. "Not really. He stole the motorcycle outside a biker bar, which was either really ballsy or really stupid. In either case, I think he'd better hope we find him before the guy who owns it does."

"What about Josiah Halftree?"

"We followed up with Ava Fairchild's cousins—the ones we could get hold of. One of them is dead now and another's in a care facility for Alzheimer's patients. The ones we talked to all got phone calls from Halftree about the jewels he claimed he saw. These are all elderly people and I don't see any of them being personally involved, but all of them say they mentioned the phone calls to other people, family and friends and whatnot. There are probably several dozen people who could have heard about it and any one of them could have connected the jewels Halftree saw to the robbery Declan was suspected of."

Death hesitated, not wanting to step on the cop's toes. "We kind of had an idea about that," he offered.

"Death did," Wren corrected. "Death's the idea man. He's the brains of the operation. I'm just the muscle." She raised her arm and made a fist, her bicep tiny next to Death's.

"Don't laugh," Death said, though he was smiling himself. "She looks harmless, but then so does that atlatl over there if you don't know what it's capable of."

Chief Reynolds laughed but didn't comment. Instead, he said, "so you had an idea, then?"

"Uh, yeah, if you don't mind my suggesting it?"

"Fire away."

"We found a secret entrance to the Campbell house. Well, Mercy Keystone found it. But we figure that's how Fairchild got in to sneak up on us when we were … uh … "

"Reading papers?" the chief suggested slyly.

"Yeah, that. Anyway, it's a lot easier way to get in than climbing through that tiny little window, so we wondered, if Whitaker was working with Fairchild, why didn't Fairchild send him in that way? And then we thought maybe Whitaker wasn't working with Fairchild after all. We thought, maybe he was working with whoever killed Josiah Halftree. If you have an idea of who Halftree talked to, and who they talked to, maybe you could check Whitaker's phone records and see if he was in touch with any of them. I mean, I know it wouldn't prove anything, but—"

"But it might give us somewhere to focus our investigation. That's a good thought. That's a real good thought." He drained his coffee and stood up. "I'm going to go get right on that. Thanks for the coffee and good luck with the hand-to-hand combat training." He started to leave, then turned back to lean over and speak to Wren in a stage whisper.

"Be careful not to damage anything you might want him to use later."

———

"There's no mention of any jewels in the will," Death said.

Wren, absorbed in the book she'd found, was still listening but distracted. "You didn't really expect there to be."

"No, I just thought it wouldn't hurt to double check. There's something about all this that bothers me. Something about the timing, or the sequence of events. Something I've seen or heard that doesn't fit in, but I just can't put my finger on it. She found the jewels in the middle of December. She found out they were the stolen jewels and not the Civil War jewels at the end of the month. She changed her will in mid-January. She died in March. What am I missing?"

"I don't know. But I'm sure you'll figure it out." She turned the page and snuffled a bit and Death turned his full attention on her. She could feel the force of his concern.

"What are you reading?"

They were sitting in the research room at the Historical Society. Millie Weeks had provided Death with their copy of Ava Fairchild's will and the table was stacked with historical documents and photographs relating to the Campbell house.

"Jenny Halifax wrote her memoirs."

"Jenny who?"

"Halifax. Remember Jenny, the slave who sat with Carolina while she was dying? Her last name was Halifax. She got it because that was where she was born. She had a daughter who was sold to another family when she was seven and Jenny never found out what happened to her. She wrote down her life story in case her daughter ever found out who she was and wondered about her past. It got published in the 1890s and the local paper reprinted it in 1976."

"Seven? God, I don't understand people. How could anyone do that to someone? The Campbells did that?"

"No, it was before she came to them. She and her family belonged to an old man who'd never married or had kids. When he died, his relatives came and sold his house and all his property at auction, including his slaves. She and her husband and daughter were all sold to different people. After the war she managed to find where her husband had gone, but he was dead. He died during a scarlet fever epidemic in the 1850s."

"Poor lady."

"You know, it's funny," Wren said. "She said she didn't learn to hate slavery until after she'd learned to be free. She was born and raised in it and she just thought that was the way things were. And she genuinely liked Carolina. Listen to this:" She took a few seconds to find her place in the book and started to read.

"When you're a slave, you don't own anything, not even yourself. Not even your child And yet, oddly enough, the one thing you can lay claim to is the person who owns you. *My* master. *My* mistress.

That's a possessive. My. Mine. Andrew never really belonged to anyone, I don't think, but Carolina was definitely mine. She was a pretty, elegant little thing, with a sense of grace and a sharp wit and an unexpected dry humor. When all the grand ladies and gentlemen gathered, for their teas and dances and cotillions, I dressed her in bright clothes and brighter jewels. I fixed her hair so that every strand was in place, and when she went in and outshone them all, I was proud. When Andrew went to war and left her lonely and frightened, I ached for her, and when she died it broke my heart."

"That's really sad. Did she say anything more in her memoirs about what happened when Carolina died? About the jewels, I mean?"

"Well, she tells the story about Carolina waking up and claiming she hid the jewels, and how, after that, she just raved incoherently. She kept talking about 'see all the pretty colors' and 'stars in the water' and 'the seventh stone'. She didn't have any idea what any of it meant. I guess, when Andrew came home, he let on that he suspected the slaves of stealing the jewelry, and there was a lot of hard feelings about it."

"Might they have taken it? I could argue that they were entitled."

"Jenny was adamant that none of them had. She said there's no way anyone could have taken the jewels before they were taken to Kansas by the abolitionists, and all the slaves who returned to the Campbells stayed in the area after the war, when they were free. Most of them worked menial jobs for very little pay and just scraped by. Certainly, none of them ever produced any fortune in jewels."

"Yeah, that makes it highly unlikely. If one of them had the jewels, they would have left to try to find someone who'd be willing to fence them and share the profits."

"Jenny was a seamstress and taught in the first black school. I gather she helped raise Andrew and Carolina's son until he was a teenager, but she never really liked Andrew and she left when the boy was old enough that he didn't need her anymore. I think she was hurt that Andrew suspected her of stealing from them, especially from Carolina. And I think she didn't think he grieved enough, and I get the feeling she didn't entirely approve of his second wife."

"Did she ever find happiness?" Death asked.

"I don't know, I haven't finished the book yet."

"Well, I hope you'll find that she did. But whatever happened, try not to grieve for it, okay? You can remember the past and you can learn from the past, but you can never change it, and the things and people it took from you are gone and will never come back. There's just no future in spending your life crying in the rear view mirror."

Wren sniffled. "You're so wise, and so reasonable and so mature," she said. "I'm going to have to beat that out of you."

FIFTEEN

"AAAAND-A-ONE-DOLLA-ONE-DOLLA-DO-I-GOTTA-ONE-DOLLA-
AND-A-ONE-AND-A-TWO-AND-A-DO-I-GOTTA-TWO-AND-A ..."

Wren kept half her attention on the item she was selling, but let
the other half roam over the crowd to find Death. He was in the side
yard, sitting in the seat of a riding mower they hadn't sold yet. He
was watching her with a faint grin and she knew he got a kick out of
listening to her drop into her patter. She also knew that he was
watching for Declan Fairchild, and if the escaped con showed his
face within a mile of this sale, Death would see him.

She turned both eyes back to the sale, kicking her speed up a
notch just to show off, and grinning to herself.

"Wren," Death had said, "has a talented tongue."

She sold three more items, glancing over from time to time to
make sure he was still there, and then she looked over and he was
gone and Jody Keystone was running and shouting.

"He took Death! He took Death! He hit him over the head and
took him!"

Death awoke to a pounding headache that sent bright flashes of light behind his eyes. For the first few seconds of consciousness he was disoriented, lost in time. He was back in Afghanistan, in the middle of a firefight with armed insurgents. Adrenaline spiked through him, ramping up his heartbeat and leaving him gasping to breathe. When he tried to dive for cover and found he couldn't move the panic nearly choked him. He fought it down, and gradually the war receded and reality returned.

It wasn't a great improvement.

He was sitting up in a hard straight chair and his hands were tied behind his back with something thin and tough but ever so slightly flexible.

He blinked his eyes open, recoiling from even the dim light in the room where he found himself. It was a kitchen, he realized. An old lady kitchen, with cat figurines on the window sill and flowery burner covers on the stove. A fine layer of dust covered everything, so an old lady kitchen that had been missing its old lady for several months.

Death's gun lay on the table, not three feet away. So close and yet still entirely out of reach. Late afternoon sun slanted through the window, more emphasizing the shadows in the room than dispelling them. The man who stood at the sink with his back to Death was a complete stranger.

Death shook his head, then wished he hadn't. Rather than clearing it, the movement sent spikes of agony shooting behind his eyes. The stranger turned with a glass in his hand and memory slowly surfaced. He'd been at the auction, looking at the mower Death was sitting on. Asking stupid questions. Acting harmless. Looking like a computer tech or an insurance adjuster. And Death had let his guard down.

"Would you like some water?" the man asked.

"Yes, please."

The stranger jerked the glass, tossing its contents in Death's face.

"Thanks."

"Don't mention it."

Death tested his bonds. Clothesline, he thought, the plastic-covered-wire kind. He had been hit over the head and disarmed and his hands were bound, but his feet were free. And he wasn't actually fastened to the chair. His arms were pulled behind his back and tied together but if he could get just a little leeway he should be able to stand up and slide free. Whoever this guy was, he was an amateur. Not that that necessarily made him less dangerous.

"So, to what do I owe the pleasure? Am I supposed to know who you are?"

"Be glad you don't," the stranger said. "It means that maybe I can leave you alive."

"I see. Unlike Josiah Halftree?"

The man just grinned. He strolled over to a cupboard beside the sink and came back with a paring knife. The faint sunlight glinted off a razor-sharp blade. "You had a gun. Didn't do you any good. You know, I've never really liked guns. But knives, now..."

Death swallowed and worked at his bonds, trying to keep his movements discreet as the cords began to loosen ever so slightly.

The stranger pulled a second kitchen chair over and Death studied the design, knowing he was probably tied to one that was identical. It was an old but sturdy-looking ladder back chair. One of them would make a passable weapon.

This second chair had a metal work light clamped to the back. The man turned it on and shone it in Death's face, making him groan and turn his head away, squeezing his eyes closed. Even through his closed eyelids, the light burned red into his aching brain.

"And now, Mr. Bogart, you're going to tell me everything you know about the jewels in the old Campbell house."

———

"Jody said it was a Mr. Ten Oeck. He substitute teaches sometimes."

The chief nodded. "Yeah, I kind of thought it might be. Death's hunch paid off. We found half a dozen calls to and from Ten Oeck on Whitaker's phone. We've been looking for him to bring him in for questioning and we've been trying to get a warrant to search his house, but the judge wasn't convinced we had reasonable suspicion and wouldn't sign off on it. He will now. Just sit tight. We're gonna find him and we're gonna get Death back for you."

Wren watched him go, angry and unhappy that she couldn't do more. She'd taken to carrying her atlatl and half a dozen darts in her truck after Fairchild shot up her house, and she fiddled with the weapon now and ached for a chance to use it.

"Ten Oeck?" she said, to no one in particular. "Who the hell is Ten Oeck, anyway?"

"Martin Ten Oeck." It was Felix Knotty who answered her. "He's Odessa Myers' grandson."

"Odessa Myers. I remember that name. From the obituary. She's one of Ava Campbell Fairchild's cousins, right?"

161

"Was, yeah. On her mother's side. She died about six months ago."

Wren narrowed her eyes, thinking fiercely. "Where did she live?"

"Old family farm, about six miles south of here."

"That's where he took Death," she said with certainty. "He's not going to take him back to his own house."

"Right. Good idea. We'll call the chief. Wren? Wren, going after him yourself is a bad idea!"

She barely paused in the act of climbing into her truck. "You want to come along?"

"Hell yeah!"

"Then get in. We'll call the cops on the way."

———

The stranger moved in slowly, brandishing the paring knife, turning it as he closed in so that the light caught and reflected back from the razor edge. It wasn't a big knife, nor anything with an impressive lineage or scary reputation. No Bowie knife, nor switchblade, nor even a Ginsu. Just a plain old kitchen knife meant for slicing apples or peeling potatoes. But Death knew that it was more than capable of scarring or even killing him.

He swallowed hard and tensed himself to action. Bad lungs or not, he had to prevail or he knew he would not be leaving this room alive.

He forced himself to breathe slowly and regularly, biding his time and waiting as the stranger moved ever closer. The ropes were loosening, but barely and slowly. They would afford him perhaps half an inch of freedom, but that would have to be enough. At the very last second, he ducked, knocked the man's knife hand away with the back of his head and then brought his head sharply forward, slamming his forehead into his assailant's nose. He felt a satisfying crunch and then the other man was reeling back, clutching his streaming nose and cursing, the knife falling forgotten to the floor.

Death rose from the chair, sliding his bound hands up the back and planting his left foot firmly on the fallen knife. As his hands cleared the top rail, he grabbed onto one of the uprights, twisted his body and swung the chair like an awkward baseball bat. *Breathe*, he told himself. *Breathe. Breathe.* His head was spinning, with spikes of pain so intense that each seemed to have its own shape and color. The room grew dim around him. He could feel unconsciousness creeping in and fought it with every fiber of his being, knowing that if he passed out before his attacker was neutralized, the best he could hope for would be to never wake up again.

The stranger roared in wordless rage and charged him like a bull, driving him back against the wall, closing his hands around Death's neck. His eyes were dark, his face twisted in fury and he was screaming out threats and insults. Death tried to ram him with his shoulders, kicked at his knees, drove one knee up into his groin. The man ignored everything he did, holding him by the throat, shaking him like a dog shaking a rat as blackness like deep water closed over his head.

———

The barn was half collapsed, the chicken house a moldering pile. A line of sheds in the back yard were gray with age and listing to one side. The yard was overgrown, but there was a van in the driveway and a light in the back. Wren circled the house, keeping close to the wall, Felix close behind her. She carried her atlatl and three darts and her slingshot and a bag full of marbles were in one pocket. The police dispatcher had warned her against approaching the house herself, but she'd pretended to lose reception and hung up.

If Death was in that house, and every instinct she had insisted he was, she'd be damned if she'd wait around for someone else to come and save him.

The sun was low in the sky now. The long grass disappeared into longer shadows. One single window in the back of the house shone yellow in the gathering twilight, and from that window there came a sudden bellow.

"You *bastard!* You goddamn utter bastard! I'm going to kill you! Do you understand? I'm going to cut you into vulture food. I'm going to take your eyes and cut out your tongue. I'm going to show you what your guts look like. I'm going to cut out your liver and *eat* it in front of you!"

There was a back door the other side of the window. Felix dropped and rolled under the window, coming up next to the door with an agility surprising in a man of his age.

"Give me some kind of distraction," he hissed.

Wren fell back several paces to give herself room. Dropping two of her darts, she set the third in the atlatl. Taking a few bare seconds to judge distance and elevation and wind speed, she drew back her arm and let fly.

———

Chaos entered the room with an explosion of glass and light and electricity as a six-foot atlatl dart crashed through the window, took out the work light and buried itself in the wall. The stranger jerked back, ducking instinctively and flinging Death away.

"What the hell?"

Death lay gasping desperately, fighting off the blackness. The knife was right in front of him, but his hands were still tied behind his back. He fought with his bonds. He could feel the wire twisting and stretching, but barely. The rope was slick with his blood and he knew that eventually he would be able to free himself, but he doubted he'd live that long.

Then the back door was yanked almost off its hinges and Felix Knotty charged in screaming "Semper Fi!"

———

"The dispatcher told you baboons not to come charging in here!"

"Did she? I couldn't understand her. It was a bad connection."

"*He* did. The dispatcher was a man tonight."

"See? I told you I had a bad connection."

Officer Grigsby rolled his eyes and thunked his head gently against the wall. His cruiser was pulled up into the farmhouse yard, its searchlight aimed through the open door. When the atlatl took out the work light, it blew every fuse in the house's 1920s-era fuse box.

"Aren't you out of your jurisdiction? Don't you have to wait for the sheriff or something?" Felix was being disagreeable, strutting around like a game cock that had been robbed of its game. Ten Oeck had bolted the minute he realized he was outnumbered. Felix had grabbed Death's gun from the table and chased after him, but hadn't even come close to catching him, a fact that wasn't helping his disposition.

"The sheriff's on his way," Grigsby said. "He's coordinating the search parties."

The police had put out a BOLO on Ten Oeck and alerted every police force within a hundred mile radius. They knew who the murderer was now, but he was still at large and no one was going to be sleeping soundly tonight.

Wren sat on the floor, cradling Death against her breast. She was petting the hair back from his face and talking baby talk to him.

"Dammit, I'm the Marine," he muttered.

She wiped his forehead with a damp cloth and leaned in close to hear him, her cheek brushing his, her long, red braid dangling over both their shoulders. "What was that?"

"I'm the Marine," he repeated. "I'm s'posed to *save* the damsel in distress. I'm not s'posed to *be* the damsel in distress!"

"Oh, honey," she said, kissing him on the temple.

There was a commotion at the kitchen door.

"I'm not letting anyone else in this building until the chief or the sheriff gets here," Grigsby said, sounding put upon.

There was a yard full of Keystones. They'd followed in Wren's wake and arrived just seconds after Grigsby did.

"You'll let Rosie through." Leona's voice was no-nonsense.

"No, I won't. I'm the cop. I'm in charge here and what I say goes. And what I say is—"

"Yes, ma'am!" Leona insisted. "You say, 'yes *ma'am*', Leroy Grigsby." She stood toe-to-toe with him in the doorway. He broke first.

"Yes, ma'am," he sighed. "But only Rosie."

He stepped aside and a slender, graceful black woman came in and knelt next to Death and Wren. "Hi, Death," she said. "I don't think we've ever been properly introduced, but I'm Rosie Keystone."

"Mercy's mom," he guessed.

"That's right. I'm also a nurse practitioner. Why don't we just take a look at you and see how you're doing?"

She shone a penlight in his eyes, one at a time, and he winced and flinched away.

"Does the light hurt?"

"Uh, a little, yeah."

"A little on a Marine scale. So that would be 'excruciating' to a normal person, right?"

He laughed slightly but didn't answer. "Who the hell is Ten Oeck?" he asked instead. "How did you find me so fast?"

"Martin Ten Oeck is a freelance accountant and substitute teacher," Wren answered. "Jody recognized him because Ten Oeck subbed in their middle school domestic engineering class last month. He's also Odessa Myers' grandson."

"Myers. Ava Fairchild's cousin. Dead or Alzheimer's?"

"What?"

He waved one hand to indicate their surroundings. "Old lady kitchen. No old lady for several months now. The chief said one of the cousins was dead and another was in a care facility with Alzheimer's. Odessa Myers. Dead or Alzheimer's?"

"Dead. About six months ago." Wren looked up at Rosie. "Even scrambled, his brains work better than most people's."

"They do. Let's see how scrambled they are." She addressed Death. "Can you tell me what day of the week it is?"

"Saturday."

"Good. Remember my name?"

"Rosie. Rosie Keystone."

"How about your full name?"

"Death Bogart."

"No middle name?"

"Not one I'm going to admit to."

"All right then." She smiled and sat back. "I think he's going to be okay. We're looking at a moderate concussion and a few bruises. Wake him up every couple of hours and make sure he's coherent. If he's not, or if you can't wake him, get him to a hospital. He needs to take it easy for the next couple of days." She turned back to Death. "I'm going to give you something for the pain, okay?"

"Thanks. You got anything for a wounded ego?"

"From what I've heard, you put up a good fight. I don't see why you think you should have a wounded ego."

"Are you kidding? I got kidnapped by a substitute home ec teacher and rescued by a girl. What the hell blew up out there, anyway?"

"Oh, that." Wren grinned. "Nothing blew up very much. Really. I just threw an atlatl dart through the window and it kind of exploded the work light. Just a little bit."

Death sighed and shook his head. "This woman's not sane, you know," he told Rosie conversationally.

"Yeah, I know."

"You're both dissing someone who throws spears at people and you claim that I'm not sane?"

"She's got a point," Rosie acknowledged wryly. "I think, if you want to keep her from atlatling anyone, your best bet is to not get kidnapped anymore."

"Yeah, because I totally did that on purpose," Death snarked.

"Well, don't do it anymore, *capisce*?"

"HUA," Wren corrected. "He's a Marine. You say 'HUA.'"

"HUA?"

"Heard, Understood, Acknowledged."

"Ah. Right. HUA, then?"

"HUA," Death agreed with a wry smile. "From now on, I promise, I will do my best to avoid any and all evil home ec teachers, substitute or otherwise."

SIXTEEN

By Rosie's decree, there wasn't anything clean enough in the old house to bandage Death's wrists, so she decided to accompany them back to Wren's place. Felix and Grigsby helped him stand and supported him out to Wren's truck. In the yard, he blinked at the sun disappearing below the treeline and shook his still-addled head.

"How late is it?"

"Not very," Grigsby told him. "We're in a valley."

With their help, he hoisted himself up into the pickup. Wren was still across the yard, talking to the sheriff, and Death took the opportunity to lean close to the older Marine.

"Man, I do appreciate the rescue, but did you really have to let Wren come along? What if she'd gotten hurt?"

Felix snorted. "I didn't let Wren come along. She let me come along. 'Course, it helped that I was the one who knew how to find this place."

"You drove?"

"Nope. She did. Like a bat out of hell."

Death just stared at him for a long minute. "You're not serious?"

Felix grinned and raised two fingers in the Boy Scout salute.

Death turned to gaze at Wren, approaching now with Rosie, and wondered what she would do if he were in a military hospital in Germany.

———

Rosie put the last piece of surgical tape around Death's wrist and pulled the coverlet up to his shoulders. "Keep him warm," she told Wren, who was perched on the edge of the bed. "Wake him up every two hours like I told you. Make sure he gets plenty of fluids and make him take the pain meds if he looks to you like he needs them. "

"Yeah," Death mumbled. "Climb under here and keep me warm, honey."

"He needs to take it easy for at least the next forty-eight hours. And just so you can't say I didn't tell you, 'take it easy' means loaf on the couch and watch game shows. 'Take it easy' does *not* mean monkey sex."

"Howsabout monkey sex on the couch while there's game shows playing in the background?"

Rosie tapped Death on the nose gently with one finger. "No monkey sex!"

"How about soft, gentle, bunny sex?" Wren suggested.

"You've obviously never seen rabbits mate," Rosie said dryly. "No sex!"

"Spoilsport," Death complained.

"I know. I'm a big meanie." She got up to take her leave. "I'll be back tomorrow to check on you. Call me if you need me."

She started for the door but stopped when Death called after her. "Hey, Rosie?"

"Yeah, sweetie?"

"Thanks for looking after me."

"You're welcome." She winked and was gone.

Wren circled the bed, crawled under the covers and pulled Death gently into her arms. "Is this okay? I want you to be comfortable."

"Mmm. S'nice." He stiffened suddenly. "Crap!"

"What's wrong?"

"Where'd my gun get to? We've got two psychos gunning for us and I'm unarmed."

"No, it's okay. It's on the nightstand. Felix gave it back." She wrapped her arms around his shoulders and squeezed him reassuringly. "I let him keep my slingshot."

"Can Felix shoot a slingshot?"

"Sure. He's the one who taught me."

"Good. That's good." He snuggled closer, appreciating the warmth and gentleness and the rare human contact. "Wren?"

"Mmm? What, sweetheart?"

"I think you'd better let me teach you to shoot. Lord knows, I'm worthless these days."

Wren was silent for a long time, long enough that he almost drifted off before she spoke. "You're not worthless," she said, and he thought she sounded like she might be crying. "You've always been the tough guy, haven't you? The big, bad Marine who solved every problem with backbone and elbow grease."

"I used to be. Once upon a time."

"And now your body keeps betraying you. And as long as you keep expecting it to behave like nothing's happened to it, it's going to keep on betraying you. I think maybe it's harder for you than you let yourself acknowledge. Soldiers who have more visible injuries are at least forced to come to some kind of terms with them. If you lose your leg, every time you look down you're going to remember that your leg is gone. But your injury is mostly invisible, so you seem to feel that you shouldn't let it affect you. That it's some sort of weakness on your part if it does."

"I'm sorry."

"Death. You have nothing to be sorry for!"

"Maybe not but … A year ago I'd have taken down Fairchild and Ten Oeck both the first time they came after me. Now, I've failed repeatedly. I can't help being ashamed of that. I'll keep trying, and I might improve, but I'm never going to be the man I once was."

"Maybe not," Wren said. "But that doesn't mean the man you're becoming won't be just as good. Or even better."

———

The A/C in the Hummer was cranked too high, overcompensating for the desert heat. They knew they were in a dangerous area and they were all four on high alert. Baker was a baby-faced newbie and twenty-three-year-old Porter was too worldly for his own good, but they were good men and they were his men, and Death had always taken care of his own.

They were driving down the main road, down what had been the only street in a now bombed-out village. They were the third vehicle in an eight vehicle convoy and, to all appearances, they were the only living souls around for miles. Then a fleeting figure appeared just on the periphery of Death's vision and rolled something into the road. There was a bright flash and a burst of noise and the Hummer flipped on a wave of heat that was partly the bomb but mostly the desert coming in through shattered windows.

He blacked out several times, but only briefly, so that the intervals of consciousness seemed like parts of a play seen under a strobe light, or the jerky, stop-motion imagery of early black-and-white films. His shirt front was covered with blood. There was pain in his chest and he was having trouble catching his breath. Barlow was trapped under the steering wheel, dangling unresponsive from his seat belt. In the back seat, Porter had an obvious head injury and Baker was incoherent, muttering with the pain of a shattered leg.

Around them, the ruins had erupted with tan-clad insurgents. Their caravan drew up into a protective circle twenty yards from where they had come to rest, and everybody was shooting at everybody else.

Death tugged at the seatbelt holding Barlow, but to no effect. Porter had a head injury and Baker's broken leg was a compound fracture. From the amount of blood he was losing, it was entirely possible that he'd taken damage to his femoral artery. Giving up on Barlow for the moment, Death got the other two out of the vehicle and, half carrying them and half dragging them, muscled them into the shelter of the circle of friendly transports.

His chest was burning, there was a fire in his lungs and oxygen seemed to be in short supply.

One of his men was still in peril.

Before anyone could stop him, he ran out into the crossfire and dived back into the wrecked Hummer. Arms caught him, circling him from behind, and he fought back without conscious thought but with deadly intent, turning on his attackers and taking them down.

"Death!" His name came out more a squeak than a shout, but it was enough to snap him out of nightmare and into a reality that held its own horrors.

He was kneeling on the floor beside Wren's bed. He had her pinned down, with one hand on her jaw and the other on her temple and he was a hair's breadth away from snapping her neck.

———

Keyed up by the day's events, Wren was still lying awake and restless when Death began to mutter and thrash. He had one hand fisted over his chest, like he was in pain, and his breathing was becoming more labored by the second. Recognizing a nightmare when she saw one, Wren moved to wake him without thinking. She wasn't even remotely prepared for his response.

He spun like a snake, grabbed her and tossed her up over his body and off the other side of the bed. It was like being caught in a tornado. She hit the floor hard with 230 pounds of muscle on top of her, his hands reaching for her head and neck. The reassuring murmur she had on her tongue came out as a barely audible squeak, but it was enough to snap him out of his dream. She could see in his eyes when he became aware of his surroundings again. Comprehension turned swiftly to shock and abject horror and he flung himself away, scrambled backward into a corner and huddled in on himself.

"No," he choked out. He was gasping and wheezing. "No. No. God, no!"

"Death?" She crawled towards him but stopped when he cowered back against the wall, one arm guarding his chest and the other flung out to ward her off. "Death, it's all right now. You're okay now. You're safe. It's fine."

"You're not safe," he countered. "I almost killed you."

"You didn't. You didn't hurt me. I'm fine. Everything's fine now."

"Nothing's fine. Don't you understand? I almost *killed* you. I almost killed you."

Wren swallowed hard. She didn't know how to handle this. "It wasn't your fault. It was my fault. It was all my fault. I know you were a soldier. I should have known better than to try to wake you up like that. I just acted without thinking. I do that a lot. But I know now and I won't do it again. I promise. It's okay."

Death pressed back into the corner, drew up his knees and wrapped his arms around them, ducking his head and hiding his face. His whole body was clenched like a fist. Stray shafts of street-light coming in the window glinted off his cheeks.

"I can't do this anymore."

"Do what?"

"This. Soldier on. Everyone I love keeps *dying.*"

"Oh, Death."

He pulled even further in on himself, which she wouldn't have thought was possible. "Even Randy," he whispered. His shoulders were shaking now, tears running free. "Even Randy's gone. He was my little brother, dammit. He was supposed to outlive me."

Wren was on her knees in front of him. She leaned toward him, reaching out one hand, but he flinched away before she even came close.

"It's going to be okay," she whispered, choking on tears of her own. "I know it's hard and I know it's scary, but you're not alone anymore. I'm not going anywhere, and I swear to you, one way or another, we are going to make things better."

———

"Spy show featuring the exploits of Napoleon Solo and Illya Kuryakin. Roger."

"What is *The Man From U.N.C.L.E.*?"

"That is correct."

"I'll take 60s television for $800"

"That's what you should do!" Wren exclaimed.

"Go on *Jeopardy*?"

"No, silly. Though I bet you're smart enough. I was talking about *The Man From U.N.C.L.E.*. I was trying to think of ways you could compensate for not being 100 percent physically. Did you ever see *The Man From U.N.C.L.E.*? It was an old spy show. They had all these nifty hidden gadgets and things tucked into their clothes and whatnot, y'know? Ink pens that were really radios and exploding tie tacks and the like."

He rolled his head along the back of the couch, turning to look at her with a minimum of effort. "What would I do with an exploding tie tack? I never even wear a tie."

She eyed him thoughtfully. "You'd look good in a tie."

They hadn't talked about what had happened the night before. Wren knew Death would just as soon pretend it hadn't happened at all. It was obvious he wasn't used to losing control, though, actually, she thought it had probably done him some good. He seemed calmer and more at ease today than he had at any time since she'd met him.

He smiled. "I don't think I even have a suit that fits anymore. If I do it's in storage."

"I said you'd look good in a tie. Who said anything about other clothes?"

"Why Miss Morgan," he teased. "Are you making a pass at me?"

"If you have to ask, it must not be a very good one."

"Any pass from you is a good one. You know what Rosie said about monkey sex, though."

"Yeah. But, you know, what Rosie doesn't know won't hurt us."

"True," a new voice said dryly from beyond the open front window. "But you're forgetting that there's *nothing* that Rosie doesn't know."

"Oops!" Wren grinned. "Hi, Rosie!"

Rosie opened the door and came in. "Am I going to have to assign you two a chaperone?"

"Nope," Death said. "We're good. Look. Couch, game show, no monkey sex."

"But I did hear the two of you talking about monkey sex."

"You didn't say we couldn't talk about it."

"True. So how are you feeling today? Any problems last night?"

They exchanged a brief glance and Wren held her silence, leaving it up to Death what to tell and what not to tell.

"I feel great," he announced with a too-bright smile. "I've been cuddled and fed and drugged and I gotta tell you, Wren's a lot better than the military on at least two of those things."

"Death Bogart," Wren said, "I'm going to be really upset if you tell me I've been out-cuddled by an army sergeant named Spike!"

Death just grinned at her and then sat patiently while Rosie changed the bandages on his wrists. "You know," he said after a minute, "it *would* be nice if I could hide some kind of knife or razor so that I could get to it if my hands were tied."

"It'd have to be a small knife. One of those little folding pocket knives, maybe?" Wren wrinkled her forehead in thought. "You know how jeans have that leather tag on the waistband, usually? Maybe if we slit the stitching on one side we could turn that into a hiding place. A pocket knife would make it bulge out, though."

"A pocket knife would," Death was grinning, "but I know what wouldn't. And I've got one in my duffel bag out in my Jeep. Which is out front," he realized suddenly. "How did it get out front? I left it at that house where the auction was."

"Yeah, and Sam took it home last night and one of his boys brought it around this morning."

"You're good, Death," Rosie told him. "You've got people behind you now. We've got you covered."

His eyes misted. "Thanks. A lot. You guys are awesome."

She flashed him a bright smile. "Yeah. We know."

Wren ran out and fetched his duffel bag, lugging it over her shoulder and staggering under the weight. "What do you have in this thing? Rocks?"

"Only a few." He hefted it up onto the sofa beside him, dug through until he found a smaller bag and extracted a tiny metal gizmo, about an inch and a half long, with a hook on one side and a hinged blade that folded out.

"Oh!" Wren exclaimed. "I have one of those!" She jumped back up from her seat the other side of his duffel bag and went to rummage through a kitchen drawer, coming back with a mate to Death's gadget. "What are they, anyway?"

"You had one and you don't know what they are?"

"I found it in a box of junk I bought at an auction."

"Of course. Well, this is a P38."

She frowned at him. "Okay, I'm not that stupid. A P38 is a plane. A great big, huge plane."

"Actually, a P38 is a small plane."

"Not that small. And, I think, less pointy."

"Yes, because the plane is a P38 Mustang fighter. *This* is a P38 hand-held can opener. They used to give them out with K-Rations and C-Rations from the second World War through Vietnam. Marines called them 'John Waynes'. No one really knows why. You don't see them much anymore. A Vietnam vet I knew gave me this. You think one of these would fit under the tag on a pair of jeans?"

"I don't know. Take your jeans off and we'll see."

Rosie gave her a stern look and Wren sighed dramatically. "Fine! I did your laundry yesterday. I'll go get a pair you're not wearing."

The tag on the jeans Wren fetched was set off-center in the back of the waistband, over the right hip. She had also brought back a small sewing kit and she hesitated over the tag with a seam ripper.

"If I cut the top seam, it's apt to gap open and someone who kidnapped you would be more likely to see it, but if I cut an end seam I'm afraid it'll fall out."

"No, go with the end seam. That should be okay. The one closest to the middle of my back. That'd be easiest to get to if my hands were tied."

"You know," Rosie said, conversationally, "it's a little alarming the way you two are casually planning for the next time he gets kidnapped and tied up. I mean, it'd be one thing if you were planning to tie one another up." She studied Death and raised one eyebrow at Wren. "I'd tie him up in a heartbeat, but you're talking about strangers doing it."

"Well," Death said, "in the past couple of weeks I've been shot at, peeping Tom'd at, and kidnapped. At this point, I figure it's best to just be prepared for anything."

"But what if they tie you up with your hands in front?" Wren asked. "What about this?" She took a tiny black disk from her sewing kit, pulled a piece of white paper from one side and stuck it to the other P38.

"What is that?"

"Peel and stick magnet."

"Okay, so ... ?"

With a bright smile, she reached over and unfastened his belt. He wore a plain belt with an oval buckle engraved USMC. She turned the buckle back and stuck the can opener to the underside, then buckled the belt back over it. "How does that feel?"

"Getting just a bit uncomfortable," he admitted.

"Oh! I'm sorry. Is the can opener poking you?"

"No." He grinned. "But the next time you unbuckle my belt, you'd better mean business."

SEVENTEEN

"Would you look at the price on those strawberries? Why is everything so expensive?"

Death glanced around, but the woman seemed to be talking to him so he shrugged and answered her. "I guess because they're out of season."

"You can get strawberries all year round."

"Well, yeah, but that's because they ship them in from, like, Mexico or Chile or somewhere. Local strawberries won't be ready until late May or June, I think."

"Hmph! Well, I still think it's highway robbery."

Death and Wren were at the local super-center, waiting on a sandwich tray from the deli. The Keystone men were setting up for a big, two-day auction of farm machinery and classic cars—things far from Wren's area of expertise. She and Death had been working at the Campbell house all morning, but stopped to take "the boys" their lunch.

Behind him, the middle-aged man stocking the produce department had greeted Wren by name.

"Hey, I just saw Eric Farrington in here," he said. "He said you and he were dating?"

"I'll kill him," Wren said. "Death, give me your gun."

"Come on, now. You know what the cops said about shooting Farrington."

She rolled her eyes. "I know. I have to wait my turn."

Glancing around, Death spotted the subject of their conversation leaning against a refrigerated floor bunker and openly ogling the young woman who was filling the milk case.

"Hey, Farrington! Get up here a minute!"

Eric stood and strolled toward them, half strutting. He was off duty and wearing jeans and a light jacket over a printed tee.

"Who do you think you are, ordering me around? I could arrest you for that. I'll have you know I'm an actual, legitimate officer of the court."

"God help the court."

"Did you tell Bob we were dating?" Wren demanded, angry.

"Oh, no. He misunderstood. I told him that you wanted to date me, but I wasn't interested."

"Eric," Death said, "not even your blow-up doll *wants* to date you."

Eric turned on Wren, who was snickering. "What are you looking at?"

"A sad little man who will never have a real girlfriend."

"That just shows what you know. I have lots of girlfriends."

"They don't count as girlfriends," Death told him, "if you have to pay them."

"I never pay them."

"They don't count as girlfriends if your mother pays them, either," Wren laughed.

"You know what? This is what I got to say to you." He pulled open his jacket and stuck his chest out at her. His tee shirt said: *I've got the dick. I call the shots.*

"Ha," she scoffed. "I squeeze the balls. I call the shots."

"Oh, really?" he sneered. He turned to Death. "Is that right, big guy? Do you let the little woman squeeze your balls?"

Death's eyes lit up and he grinned a huge, face-splitting grin. He put an arm around Wren's shoulders and pulled her close.

"Oh, *yeah!*"

———

"Okay, so I know the John Deere is the yellow and green one. Was the blue one the Ford and the orange the Allis-Chalmers?"

Roy Keystone stopped beside Wren and looked over her shoulder at the list she was making on her laptop. "You know, we really can handle this, honey, if you want to go back to the Campbell house with that pretty new boyfriend of yours."

She smiled at him. "I would, but he got a call from one of the local bail bondsmen and he thinks he might have a job lined up. He lives pretty close to the line, you know?"

"Yeah, I know. But at least he doesn't have to sleep in his car anymore, right?" Roy grinned.

"You know about that?" She'd been dying to talk that over with someone, but out of respect for Death's feelings, she hadn't mentioned it to anyone.

"Small town. Word gets around. Don't tell my wife I admitted this, but a bunch of old men gossiping will put a bunch of old women to shame any day." He leaned down and tapped her computer screen. "The 'plow-ey thing with pulleys and buckets' is a cultivator."

"I knew that …"

———

Death tapped on the door and let himself in when the voice inside invited him to. He found Warren Hagarson seated behind his desk. Hagarson was a tall, stout man with black hair going gray and a jovial smile that didn't always reach his eyes. He had company just now, Death realized. A nervous teenager with a bad case of acne sat across from him in the hard plastic chair.

"Ah, Mr. Bogart," Hagarson said. "Come in! Come in. Bogart, this is Ethan. Ethan tried to rob a convenience store. Not real successfully. Ethan, Mr. Bogart is a bounty hunter. Show him your license, Bogart."

Death obligingly pulled out his license and held it up in front of the kid's face.

"Oh, that's okay," Ethan stammered. "I don't need to—Death?! Your name is Death?"

Death gave him a merry smile and didn't bother to correct the pronunciation.

"And he works for me," Hagarson said.

"Ah, yeah." Death let the smile drop away, rubbed the back of his neck and feigned nerves of his own. "Um, what was the penalty again if I brought you someone and they weren't, you know, actually breathing anymore?"

Hagarson put his hands up. "Bogart! Again? What happened this time?"

"Man, it totally wasn't my fault! He was resisting arrest."

"How?"

"He hid from me. Plus, he was whining. It was really annoying."

Hagarson sighed. "Well, I hope it was worth it. Like I told you last time, dead bodies only fetch half the bounty." He looked over at Ethan. "You have to be patient with Mr. Bogart. He's a bit testy. You're not going to make me send him after you, are you?"

"No, sir! Never, sir! Absolutely not, sir!"

"Good. Then get out of here and I will see you in court," he consulted some papers, "a week from Thursday. Got it?"

"Yes, sir!"

Hagarson nodded and Ethan made a run for it. They stood in silence until the outer door closed behind him.

"You think he really bought that?" Death asked.

Hagarson sniffed. "Oh, yeah. I wouldn't sit in that chair if I were you."

Death laughed and seated himself on the corner of the desk. "I was a little surprised to hear from you. I'd heard that you always handle your own skips."

"Usually I do." Hagarson pushed his chair back and put his right foot up on the desk. It was in a cast. "Tripped over my wife's pet rat."

"Your wife has a pet rat?"

"She calls it a chihuahua."

"Ah. I see. So what do you need from me?"

"You captured Tyrone Blount last week."

"Yeah."

"Well, I bailed him out again. He secured the bond with a truck, title and all. Only now the truck's been reported stolen. Thief broke into a house while the family was away, stole a bunch of papers out of a wall safe, including the title to the truck in the driveway, then stole the truck on their way out."

"Blount," Death said, voice flat. "And then he used the stolen truck as security for a bail bond. And he didn't think this would come back to bite him in the ass?"

"Never said the man was a genius. You brought him in once. Think you can find him again?"

"I'd certainly be willing to try."

———

The farm equipment auction wasn't until the weekend, but there was a lot of work to do to get ready. It was going to be one of the Keystone's biggest sales of the year. Wren worked beside the family, cleaning, cataloging, double-checking inventories and planning the logistics of the auction. In the bustle of activity, no one paid much attention to the narrow, two-lane blacktop that ran by the sale sight, nor to the fallow field across the road, and certainly not to the weathered old barn that stood in the center of that field. If they had been paying attention they might have seen a hint of movement in the old hay mow, the outline of a shadowy figure or the glint of sunlight on a binocular lens.

———

The problem with Blount, as Death already knew, was that he was paranoid. He was always on alert and he'd run at the drop of a hat. He lived in a ramshackle old two-story house on top of a high hill that gave him a clear view of the road. He claimed he couldn't work because he had a bad back, but Death had seen him jump from the second-floor window and run for the next road over, half a mile away through deep woods. He was part of a community of low-lifes that haunted the county, a loose affiliation of petty thieves and drug dealers, and there always seemed to be someone he could call on to help him get away.

This time Death didn't bother to drive up to the house first. He pulled into the driveway of an abandoned homestead, hid his jeep behind a massive lilac bush, and hiked down to the creek that separated Blount's property from the rest of the world.

Last time he'd gone after Blount, Death had tried to ambush him in these woods, but he hadn't taken his own health into account and had come off the worse for wear. He still thought this was a good place to stop him, though. There were a hundred paths through the woods, but only three places to cross the creek.

From his time in the Corps, Death knew a dozen different booby traps. He wracked his brain now, trying to come up with one that wasn't lethal. The three paths across the creek consisted of a shallow ford, a line of stepping stones, and a downed tree that formed a makeshift bridge. He could, of course, booby trap all three, but he felt his chances of success would increase if he could eliminate two of the options, funneling Blount into a bottleneck of his own choosing.

The ford was the simplest and most straightforward route across the stream and would be the hardest to sabotage, but it would also be the worst place to set a trap. The path down the bank was narrow but too steep to safely trap anyone. Blount was a criminal and a creep and a fool, but Death still didn't want to hurt him.

He studied the path leading down to the ford. He could dig it out a little without too much exertion, but it was already nearly vertical, and a man who'd jump out a second-story window wouldn't hesitate to jump six feet. On the opposite side of the stream, the ground rose eight feet or more in a steep bluff, concave at some places and impossible to climb. The only way up was to follow a gully, where runoff from years of rainstorms had worn a path down to bedrock. At the head of the gully... Death looked up and smiled.

A massive tree loomed over him, once majestic but now dead and listing toward the creek. The scar of a lightning strike snaked down one side. Its roots had lost their grip on the soil and erosion had begun to carve a cave beneath it. It was only a matter of time until the ancient forest giant gave in to gravity and fell.

With a backpack full of supplies over his shoulder, Death crossed the creek and carefully climbed the gully, circling the tree gingerly, lest it topple before he was ready for it to. Once he was safe on the opposite side, he took a small hand saw from his pack and cut through the three largest roots still anchoring the tree. A smaller fallen tree served as a fulcrum and a long limb made for an effective lever. He wedged the lever under the edge of the dead tree and threw his full weight against the other end, and with a deep groan and a mighty crash, the old tree fell.

The tree's corpse filled the gully, crossed the creek and blocked the path on Blount's side as well. To clear the tree away, or even fashion it into another bridge that could be used, would require days of work with a heavy-duty chainsaw.

It had been a noisy operation, and Death could well imagine that the sound of the tree falling would attract the attention of the paranoid and hyper-vigilant man at the top of the hill. He stayed out of sight behind the upthrust root ball. After some ten minutes of waiting, his excess caution paid off.

Blount was a good woodsman, Death had to give him that, but Death had no trouble spotting the smaller man and following his progress down the hill. Blount moved cautiously, sticking to cover and watching warily for any sign of an intruder. He saw the fallen tree and blocked path and hesitated, studying the situation. His mouth was moving, *talking to himself*, Death thought. He was too far away to read his lips, but he could tell, from Blount's body language, the exact second he gave it up as an act of God. Coming out of hiding, he looked the fallen tree over one last time and then casually made his way back up the hill.

When he was safely out of sight, Death made his own way upstream to the northernmost crossing, the steppingstones. Here, five irregularly-spaced boulders made a hopscotch pattern across a wide section of the stream where the water ran swift and deep. Death had brought his lever with him and as he crossed he shifted each stone behind him, so that they no longer formed a usable path.

That left only the fallen log, and here he would set his trap. Hidden from suspicious eyes on the hillside by the rising bank behind him and the thick branches overhead, he dropped his pack on the sandy shore. Kneeling beside the near-end of the log, he reached under with his cupped hands and began to scoop out a shallow depression.

"Hello?" Wren stood up, pressed her phone closer to her ear and walked away from the massive combine she was scrubbing. "No, I'm sorry. You're breaking up. I can hardly hear you … Death? Death's not here. What? What … sorry? Death? Oh, this is Death? Is this you? I'm sorry, I can barely hear you. What? You want me to … what? Go where? Meet you? The Campbell house? Okay. Okay. I'll be right there."

She hung up the phone and returned it to her pocket. "I need to go," she told Doris, who was working next to her. "Death wants me to meet him at the Campbell house. He says he thinks he has an idea."

"Okay, honey. Go on and have fun. Don't do anything I wouldn't like to do."

EIGHTEEN

TYRONE BLOUNT LIVED ON the barter system. The three downstairs rooms in the house he claimed (but did not actually own) were filled to bursting with a random assortment of things he had collected to trade. There was furniture—none of it the antiques he boasted of—old appliances, car parts, bits and pieces of mowers and garden equipment, dishes, knickknacks, jars of coins, books of stamps, and other ephemera too strange and too varied to detail.

The sole upstairs room, more an attic really, held an old army cot, a broken-down recliner, a third-hand television with a battered VCR, and a collection of much-watched porn videos. He had a small refrigerator and an electric burner where he cooked things that could either blow up or put him in prison for life if his luck ever turned really bad.

There were long windows to the east and west and a pair of dormer windows facing south. The north wall was originally a blind spot, but with the ingenuity of the truly paranoid, Blount had drilled out a small, circular hole and inserted the scope from a deer rifle. He fitted it with a rubber bushing so he could move it around to sweep the horizon.

He was lounging in his chair, drinking a beer and watching his favorite titty flick when he heard the sound of a motor. Setting the beer down, he sidled up to the west window, standing beside it so he could peer out without making himself a target. A silver-gray Jeep was making its way up his driveway, and he immediately recognized it as belonging to the bounty hunter who'd caught him last time.

With a sharp curse, he ran across the room, wrenched open the east window, lowered himself until he was hanging by his fingertips, and dropped to the ground. With a little luck the guy would stop to search his maze of a house first. By the time he realized Blount wasn't there, Tyrone could be miles away, drinking beer with one of his buddies and laughing about how stupid the law and its minions were.

He loped easily down the hill, the steep grade increasing his speed. The woods began two-thirds of the way down. Instinctively, he took the path for the ford, but at the last minute he remembered that the lightning-blasted tree had fallen and blocked the way. Hesitating for only an instant, he turned right and followed a less well-traveled trail.

He ran across the narrow shelf between the bottom of the hill and the top of the deeper hollow that the creek had worn through the valley. Up a slight rise and then down a gentle slope and he came out in a small clearing where an older fallen tree made a sturdy bridge across the water.

He stepped on the end of the bridge and it gave beneath him, bouncing a little. There was a swift rustling in the grass and a loop of rope came up and closed around his ankles, drawing tight. He braced himself, expecting to be swung off his feet into the trees like in the movies, but the rope merely tightened and stopped. One end ran off to his left and was knotted around a tree. The other ran up and disappeared into the branches overhead.

Tyrone Blount shook his head in disbelief. Rope? The guy thought he could catch him with rope? Really?

"It didn't work, dumbass!" he yelled into the surrounding woods. "You hear me? Your lame-ass trap didn't work!"

Pulling a knife from his pocket, he leaned down and cut the rope. The loose end shot up, there was a rustling, rushing sound, and before he could even straighten up, the weight of a falling cargo net dropped him face-first into the loam.

———

Wren pulled up and parked in the Campbell house driveway. She looked around, but there was no sign of Death. Getting ready for the big auction had been hot, dirty work. She considered going home to shower and change, but she didn't want to keep Death waiting. There was a pack of antibacterial wipes in the glove compartment, so she settled for wiping off her face and arms and the back of her neck. She shook her long, red hair out and re-braided it neatly into the trademark plait she wore down her back. Dusting off her blouse and jeans, she decided she'd do.

The Campbell house really was a beautiful old building. Spring sunlight shone down. The clapboard siding was very white in the light, the slate roof tiles very dark in comparison. Sunshine reflected off dusty stained glass in the oriel windows that circled the tower, contrasting the brightness of the day without and the shadows of the house within. A flag pole was set in brackets from the pillar that braced the roof of the verandah to the left of the main steps. An

American flag flew from it now, hanging limp in the late-afternoon stillness.

Once, she knew, that same flagpole had held the Confederate banner.

Wren climbed the steps and stopped. There was a single purple iris taped to the door, a piece of paper wrapped around the stem. She took down the flower and smelled it appreciatively. She loved the scent of irises, not so much a perfume, really, but a light, earthy scent that she associated with spring and green and growing things.

She unrolled the paper and found it covered with a sloppy scrawl.

Wren,

Come look in the secret entrance.

Love, Death.

With a bright smile and a spring of anticipation in her step, she unlocked the door and went in. Her footsteps rang on the wooden floor as she crossed to the morning room. The window seat looked just as it had the last time she'd seen it. Clutching her flower and already grinning, she released the catch that Death had installed and lifted the lid.

Declan Fairchild sat up and pointed a gun in her face.

She stumbled back, dropped the flower and turned to run. *If someone pulls a gun on you, run,* Death had told her. *If you run, he might not shoot. If he shoots, he might not hit you. If he hits you, it might not be serious. If you just give in, you're dead.*

She almost made it to the hall, but Martin Ten Oeck stepped into view, blocking the doorway. His nose was still swollen and red from his fight with Death, and twin black eyes, fading now to mustard yellow, gave him the look of a deranged raccoon. He was smiling brightly and toying with a knife. She heard Fairchild approaching from behind, heard the scuffle of soft shoes on parquet and felt a presence. Then something struck her on the back of the head and she fell into darkness.

———

Death drove around Blount's house and eased his Jeep off the dirt driveway and into the grassy field to the east. He knew from experience that Blount would resist, and he wasn't dragging the little twerp any farther than he absolutely had to. He parked where the line of trees began and strolled casually down the hill. There was no need to hurry. If his trap had worked, Blount wasn't going anywhere. If it hadn't, he'd have to start over again anyway.

He heard his quarry cussing before he topped the rise that overlooked the creek and grinned in satisfaction.

Blount was stretched face-down under the heavy cargo net. He had a small pocket knife, but the weight of the net pinned him in such a way that he couldn't move more than the tips of his fingers. He was sawing away at one of the strands, but couldn't get enough force behind the blade to make a dent. It would take him hours, at the least, to cut his way out of this predicament.

Figuring that his prisoner would be easier to handle if he exhausted himself, Death had come prepared to wait. Seating himself on the grassy bank, he swung a backpack off his shoulder and pulled out a sub sandwich and a bottle of water. This really was a lovely place for a picnic. Tiny violets dotted the grass like stars, dappled shadows moved over his skin as the trees tossed in a light breeze and the shallow creek burbled and sang across the rocks.

"Let me know when you're ready to come quietly," he said. "There's no hurry. I brought lunch." He took a healthy bite of his sandwich and washed it down with a drink of water. When his mouth was empty he addressed Blount casually. "So, you secured your bail with a stolen truck. Were you really expecting that to work out for you, or are you just trying to get on one of those stupid criminal shows?"

Blount cursed colorfully. "You just wait, you dirty sonofabitch! I'm gonna knock your goddamn head off. I'm gonna cut your balls off and shove 'em down your throat. I'm gonna kill you!"

Death took his phone out. He had no reception out here, down in this hollow, but phones can be used for other things. "Sorry, could you repeat that?" he asked Blount.

Blount obliged.

Death clicked the phone off and tucked it back in his pocket. "Thanks. You do realize I'm going to give this to the DA?"

"You can't do that! You ain't read me my rights!"

"Um, yeah. Not a cop, remember? As far as I'm concerned, you don't have any rights. I suppose I could make some up for you." He thought about it while he ate. "You have the right to be a moron."

"What are you, some kind of comedian?"

"If you could choose to give up the right to be a moron, we both wouldn't be here. If you decide to exercise your right to be a moron, you can and will get your ass kicked."

Death finished his lunch and his bottle of water, tucked his trash carefully back into his backpack and looked at his watch. He stood and stretched. "Right," he said. "I think that's enough now. I want to get you back to town in time to get paid tonight."

He went over to the trapped man, set his foot on Blount's fingers, and took the knife from him. Working through the spaces in the net, he handcuffed the man's wrists together behind his back and tied a short length of rope around his ankles, hobbling him so that he could not run away. This was going to be the tricky part. He couldn't get the Jeep any closer and he knew that he wasn't physically capable of dragging Blount up the hill. He needed to get him on his feet and keep him on his feet and moving forward.

He hunted around the underbrush until he came up with a couple of long, sturdy sticks. Then he carefully rolled back the netting, exposing only Blount's left leg. He shoved one of the sticks up his jeans leg where it reached about halfway up his thigh. Then he tied it down at the top and the bottom, so that it kept Blount from bending his knee. He repeated the process with the other leg, then folded the net back the rest of the way and used more of the rope to fashion a harness around his chest.

"What the hell are you doing?" Blount demanded.

"Controlling you."

The sticks fastened to his legs like splints would keep him from folding up and sitting down, forcing Death to carry or drag him. The harness would allow Death to keep him from falling forward with minimal effort and Death would walk behind him, so he couldn't fall backwards.

Getting behind Blount, Death levered him to a standing position, then just stood a minute until he got his breath back under control. "Okay, now. March!"

"Make me."

Death stooped and picked up another stick. He was developing a real fondness for sticks. Without a word, he poked it into the back of Blount's right knee. Blount jerked reflexively and staggered forward, kept upright only by the rope harness Death held.

"You can walk without getting poked or you can walk because of getting poked. It's entirely up to you."

The trip up the hill was tedious and awkward, but uneventful. You couldn't even really count Blount's cursing, Death thought. He had a foul mouth, to be sure, but he lacked the range and inventiveness that Death, as a Marine, had come to expect from a good cussing out.

Getting him into the Jeep was tricky. He put a folded tarp on the passenger seat before levering Blount up and in, remembering Ethan in Hagarson's office. He made him sit sideways while he quickly removed the splints from his legs, then spun him around and fastened the seat belt across his torso, leaving his hands cuffed behind his back this time.

Death's cargo net was still back in the woods, but he would come back for that later. Circling the vehicle, he climbed into the driver's seat and turned the nose up the hill, in high spirits.

"You don't have to be so cheerful," Blount snapped peevishly.

"I've got every reason to be cheerful," he said. "I've got a job well-done, a paycheck waiting and a pretty girl to spend it on."

———

Wren awoke slowly. At first the only thing she was aware of was that she was uncomfortable. She blinked slowly and her head pounded, starbursts of light exploding behind her eyes. When she tried to reach a hand up to her aching forehead she couldn't move it. Thin stripes of pain closed across the back of her wrists, like too-tight bracelets. Her stomach roiled, but there was an uncomfortable force across her face and she couldn't open her mouth.

Breathing through the nausea, she took her time, sitting quietly with her eyes closed until her stomach steadied and the headache subsided. Cautiously, she cracked her eyelids open again, waited while her pupils adjusted to the light level, and then blinked the room into focus.

She was still in the Campbell house, in the Naked Dead Guy Parlor, but the chair she was sitting in had come from the dining room. It was one of the straight-backed upright dining chairs—one of the ones with arms that had stood at the head and foot of the table. Her wrists were strapped to the arms with plastic zip ties. She could feel similar restraints around her ankles, though she couldn't see how they were tied. Something was looped around her waist, tying her to the chair back, and there was a strip of duct tape across her mouth.

Footsteps approached and she turned her head frantically, trying to see who was coming and from where. It took her addled brain several seconds to realize that the sound came not from behind her, but from in front of her and overhead. Two sets of footfalls were descending the circular staircase.

"So this is where my little friend Flow bought it," Declan Fairchild observed, casually. "Why on earth did you involve him, anyway?"

"He was a fence. I figured he'd know how to sell the jewels if we found them. And I thought maybe you'd told him where you hid them." Ten Oeck followed him.

Fairchild snorted. "Obviously you don't know me very well."

Ten Oeck was still playing with a knife, a butcher knife this time, its edge gleaming in the late afternoon sunlight. "Just so long as you know me," he said meaningfully.

Fairchild had reached the bottom of the stairs and now he turned his attention to Wren. "Oh, look! Our little bird's awake." He came over to her, openly studying her face, letting his eyes roam over her body. He reached out and flipped loose the top three buttons on her blouse, baring the upper part of her bra, and leaned in to look down her shirt.

She shuddered and gagged behind the duct tape.

Fairchild loomed over her, straddled her suggestively. "You know, I was in prison for a long, long time."

She leaned back, trying to put space between them.

He bent down and whispered in her ear. "Don't worry. I'm not going to do anything to you. Yet. I want to wait until I have an audience."

She glanced fearfully at Ten Oeck and Fairchild laughed derisively and stood up. "Oh, him. He wouldn't be any fun. He's not interested in anything but cutting things. Though, he really *does* like cutting things. Don't you Marty?"

Ten Oeck smiled a creepy smile and walked around behind her, out of her line of sight. He laid one hand on her shoulder and his knife appeared in the corner of her vision.

"Oh, yeah. I like cutting things. I like cutting things a lot."

———

Death swung down out of his Jeep and headed for Wren's door with a bouquet of flowers in one hand and a grocery bag in the other. He paused to speak to Lucy and Thomas, but didn't try to pet either of them, laden as he was. It took some fumbling to get out the key she'd given him and let himself in. When he did, he was surprised all over again by the sudden, welcome feeling of "home" that surrounded him.

It sent a bittersweet pang through him, to the roots of his soul. He *wanted* this. He'd been so lonely for so long and this, a welcoming home and a warm woman to share it with, was everything he'd been dreaming of. He wanted it, but, for so many reasons, he didn't dare reach for it.

He wanted to talk to Randy. In all the months since his brother had died, he'd never yet missed him with such a powerful longing.

Randy had been his sounding board. Death could share anything with him, and Randy would put it into perspective, give him whatever he needed, be it a pat on the shoulder or a kick in the ass.

Without mentioning it to anyone, Death had swallowed his pride earlier and called the VA to ask for psychiatric counseling. The woman had put his name on a waiting list. He hadn't asked, but he had a feeling it was a long list. He wondered how long Wren would let him hold her at arm's length before she gave up on him and walked away.

Wren's truck was not out front and he figured she was probably still out at the auction site with the Keystones. He put her flowers in a vase with water, set a tub of gourmet ice cream in the freezer, and put a bottle of wine in the refrigerator to chill. He had just mixed up a marinade and put the two steaks he bought in it when Lucy set off on a sudden fit of angry barking.

Frowning, he put the steaks in the refrigerator, wiped his hands on a towel and went to the front door.

Lying on the top porch step was a clear plastic bag containing a sheet of paper and what looked, at first, like a coiled snake. He leaned down to look closer, then picked up the bag, his heart pounding in his chest and his blood running cold.

It was Wren's long, red braid, hacked off with a knife.

With shaking hands he opened the bag and pulled out the paper and read the words printed there.

The old Campbell house. Come alone. Come unarmed. No cops. You have twenty minutes and then we start finding other things to cut off.

Tick. Tock.

NINETEEN

THE LAST TIME DEATH saw his grandmother was the day he left for his last deployment.

Death sped down the narrow back street, taking the most direct route he knew, completely ignoring speed limits. A small kitten was sunning itself in the middle of the street. It started when it saw his Jeep bearing down on it and dashed for the sidewalk, barely avoiding his rushing wheels. He was glad that it got out of the way. If he'd hit it, he would have felt bad, but he wouldn't have stopped.

He knew how Wren had felt, driving like a bat out of hell.

He pulled the Jeep into the park next to the Campbell house, turned it off and practically fell out of it in his haste. A tall wooden fence ran around the perimeter of the park. Unless Wren's captors (the note had said "we") were watching from the second floor, he should be hidden from them. Keeping a low profile and ignoring the strange looks he was getting from a couple of young mothers over by the playground equipment, he crossed the park at a run and circled the fence to come at the Campbell house from the back, at an angle overlooked by only the tiny window in the pantry.

The last care package he'd gotten from his parents had arrived in the mail the same morning they were killed.

His heart was pounding, his head spinning and he found himself gasping for air. Only force of will and the knowledge that Wren was counting on him allowed him to slow down for two precious minutes and just breathe. When he could see again and the gasping had subsided, he dropped down and belly-crawled across the lawn to come out under the verandah.

He paused to look at his watch. He had eleven minutes, if they were true to their word.

The ground under the verandah was dry and dusty. It hadn't seen direct rain in well over a century and a half. He had to crawl clear around the house, keeping his head down so he didn't knock against the floorboards and alert them that he was under here. On his left side, wooden lattice supported the lower branches of climbing roses and sweet pea and morning glory. The house was on his right. The foundation was made of big, rough-cut stones, a mixture of limestone and sandstone by the look of it. They were joined by thick strips of discolored mortar.

On the east side, under the morning room, he found the sliding panel that led to the secret entrance. He looked at his watch. He had eight minutes to go.

Crawling under the house, Death held his breath. He listened for any sound that would tell him anything, but everything was silent as a tomb. He found the place where the end of the window seat opened and pushed it in carefully. Gently, ever so gently, desperate to not be heard, he took his gun from his belt, made sure the safety was off, and slid it into the window seat. His phone followed. Then he closed the secret door and backed away.

He Skyped with Randy last thing before he left on his final mission, never dreaming that within 48 hours his brother would be dead.

He backed out from under the house, back out to the run beneath the verandah, and headed for the nearest opening. According to his watch, he had five minutes.

Death left the cover of the verandah and ran for the nearest bushes in the Campbell house's old, overgrown flower garden. He circled and came at the place from the front, not trying to hide now and not trying to disguise that he was sweating and out of breath.

The porch steps sounded hollow under his tread. There was no movement at any of the windows and no sign of any kind of life inside.

When he told Wren goodbye that morning, he'd never imagined that he might not see her again.

He pounded on the Campbell house door. "I'm here, dammit! Fairchild? Is that you? I'm here. Don't hurt her! Don't you hurt her. I came just like you asked me to. Are you there, Fairchild? I'm here!"

There was a step in the foyer and Death braced himself and waited for the door to open.

It swung inward. Death could sense two bodies waiting in the shadows. The door opened all the way back and he could see the entire entry hall except for two little slices hidden by perspective, one on either side of the door. Then his eyes fell on the parlor door, which also stood open.

Wren was in the parlor—the Naked Dead Guy Room, she called it. She was tied to a straight chair and there was a strip of duct tape over her mouth. Her blouse was half open and her face red from crying. Her ravaged hair stood out around her head, making her look both vulnerable and wild.

"Don't hurt her," he said. "Just don't hurt her. You can do anything you want to me, but, I'm begging you, please! Don't hurt her!"

———

Death stood in the doorway and he looked scared. He was slightly gray and sweating, dusty and disheveled and there was a wheeze in his voice when he spoke. Wren wanted nothing so much as to take him in her arms and comfort him, promise it would be okay. But her arms were still tied tight to the chair and any promise she could have given him at this point would have been a lie.

Fairchild stepped out on the porch behind him, out of her line of vision, just for a second.

"Where's your car?" he demanded when he came back in.

Death tipped his head toward Wren's house. "Three blocks that way. Ran out of gas."

Fairchild thought about it and apparently decided to accept that as truth. He swung the door closed and motioned with the gun. "Put your hands above your head and go into the parlor. I want you over by the stairway. Try anything stupid I'll shoot you, and then I'll let Ten Oeck start carving up your girlfriend."

Death raised his hands and moved forward cautiously, coming into the room.

"You okay?" he asked her as he passed.

She nodded, still silenced by the duct tape, and Fairchild kicked Death in the back of the knee.

"No talking! I'll tell you when you can talk."

They put Death against the inner curve of the stairway, brought his hands down and she heard the high rattling noise as they fastened a plastic zip tie around them.

"Search him," Fairchild told Ten Oeck. "See if he's carrying or wired."

Ten Oeck searched him thoroughly, but Death ignored the man and just stared at Wren. He seemed to be drinking in the sight, memorizing her. She met his eyes, tried to offer him some measure of reassurance. It would have been easier if she'd believed herself that everything would be okay.

Fairchild quickly lost patience. "Is he clean or not?"

Ten Oeck stood up. "He's clean."

"Yeah, good." Fairchild sounded bored. "Here, hold my gun."

"I don't like guns."

"For Pete's sake! Just hold the damn thing!"

Ten Oeck reluctantly took the gun and wandered back to stand by Wren. Fairchild spun suddenly and drove his fist into Death's stomach.

Death rocked back against the railing as Fairchild hit him again and again. Wren struggled against her bonds, sobbing. Fairchild moved up to slug Death in the jaw and the Marine shook his head and spat out blood.

"What the hell are you doing?"

"Just softening you up, tough guy."

Ten Oeck watched dispassionately. "I could get him to talk faster," he offered.

"Yeah," Fairchild said sarcastically. He was panting with the exertion of the beating he was delivering and he staggered away from Death now, wiping his forehead. "And then you get carried away and sever the carotid or the femoral artery and he goes and bleeds out before we learn anything. You see? This is why you never accomplish anything."

Death's left eye was swelling. He had a cut on his mouth and a bruise was already darkening his jawline. He glared at the two men. "Just what is it you think that I can tell you, anyway?"

"I think you know," Fairchild said. He paced around the room once, then turned again to his captives. "Look, there's two ways we can do this. I can torture you to make her talk, or I can torture her to make you talk. Frankly, I prefer the first option, because I have much better plans for her, but I'm flexible, you know. So here's the question, and I don't care which one of you answers me." He went back over to Wren and ripped the duct tape from her mouth, then glared at them, first one and then another.

"What did you do with my goddamn jewels?"

TWENTY

"WE NEVER HAD YOUR jewels!" Death answered. Wren was sobbing too hard to talk, half from the fear and the grief for Death's injuries and half from a blinding, blood-red rage.

"I'm not stupid," Fairchild snarled. "I know where I hid them. I came back to get them and they were gone, and your girlfriend here was the only one who'd been in the house."

"Okay, first of all, we never even knew that compartment existed until we found it after you left it open. Second, Wren wasn't even remotely the only person who'd been in the house. Look around you. You see all those dust covers we pulled off the furniture? Someone came in and put them on everything after your aunt died. Someone came in and cleaned out the refrigerator and got clothes for her to be buried in. More recently, there've been members of the Historical Society, representatives of a dozen different auction companies that posted bids for the sale contract, and a small army of law enforcement officials, after your buddy Flow went and broke his neck here."

"So you're saying that one of them took my jewels instead of you?"

"No, because if you look in that empty compartment, you'll see that there's a thick layer of dust with nothing disturbing it except for your hand print."

Fairchild scoffed. "There's ways to fake a thick layer of dust."

Death frowned, disbelieving. "Like what?"

"Like, dust it around with a powder puff. Or fill a baster with dust and blow it into the compartment. Or run a vacuum cleaner with no filter and angle it so the exhaust goes in there."

"And you really think that someone who's found a cache of priceless jewels is going to bother with something like that instead of just taking them and getting the hell out of Dodge?"

Ten Oeck, leaning casually against Wren's chair and cleaning his fingernails with the butcher knife, glanced over at her and spoke conversationally.

"And he thinks I'm the unstable one."

She stared at him.

"You cut people with knives for fun."

"Well, yeah. There is that."

"You do realize," Fairchild said, "that if you don't have my jewels, I really don't have any reason to keep you alive."

"You don't have any reason to kill us, either."

"I don't really need a reason. You're annoying and I don't like you. That's reason enough for me. Anyway, I think you're lying." He walked over and looked Death straight in the eye. "I think you know exactly where my jewels are."

Death returned his gaze. "Listen to me. In the last three years, I've lost my whole family. My career, my health, my wife, my home. All my plans, all my goals. Everything I had. Everything I was. All my hopes and all my dreams. The only good thing I have left in the whole world is that woman sitting there, and I would do anything—*give* anything—to protect her."

Fairchild just stared for a long minute. "Oh, stop," he said finally. "You're breaking my heart." He paced around in a small circle, then shook his head. "Nope. Nope. I don't buy it. Those jewels are worth *millions*. You could buy all the girlfriends you want."

"You can't buy girlfriends!"

He raised his eyebrows. "Really? I've always bought mine."

"Look," Death tried again, "we don't have your jewels. But we know who took them and we think they're still here, and if you give us a chance, maybe we can help you find them."

———

When they'd backed Death up to the banister, they'd pulled his arms down on the staircase side and fastened them together, tied to one of the balusters with a zip tie. He could feel the open edge of the leather tag on the back of his jeans, but he didn't dare work at getting the P38 free while he was the focus of their attention. On the other hand, he didn't want them focusing on Wren either. He needed them distracted and he needed time.

"What do you mean, you know who took them? And if someone took them, why would they still be here?"

"Because it was your aunt who found them, and she hid them again."

"That dotty old woman? She couldn't find her own ass with both hands."

Death wanted to slap himself in the forehead or thunk his head against the nearest wall. "Tell me something. How long have the two of you been working together?"

Fairchild and Ten Oeck glanced at one another and shrugged.

"Since this afternoon," Ten Oeck said.

"Aunt Ava and Uncle Fred had a cabin at the lake," Fairchild said. "We used to go there for Fourth of July when we were kids. I was out there using it as a hideout when Martin showed up wanting to use it as a hideout."

"I see. And have you talked at all?"

"Well," this time it was Ten Oeck who answered. "We considered killing each other, but then we thought we'd have a better chance of finding the jewels if we work together."

"And then you can always kill each other later?"

"Probably," Fairchild agreed easily. "But if you're trying to play us against each other, you're wasting your time. You want us to think we can't trust one another. Well, we don't trust one another now. We're good with that."

"You have a really charming family dynamic," Death said, "but that wasn't my point. Ten Oeck—Martin—why did you kill Josiah Halftree?"

"I didn't mean to!" he replied at once. "That was an accident! You can't hold me responsible for that. It was totally not my fault."

"You stabbed him seventeen times."

"I got a little … carried away."

"Okay, but why did you grab him in the first place?"

"He called me up, asking about Ava's jewels. He said he knew she had some really valuable pieces, and if whoever inherited them wanted to sell them, he wanted to help."

"Did he say anything else?"

Ten Oeck thought about it. "No! No! God, no! Please, don't! Aaaaahhhhhh!"

212

Death rolled his eyes. "Anything about why he thought Ava had valuable jewels?"

"Oh, that. He said because she showed them to him. She brought them in thinking they were the lost jewels from the Civil War, but when he told her they were too modern she said she must be getting senile and had forgotten buying them."

"You see?" Death asked Fairchild. "Your aunt was looking for the Campbell family jewels and she found the ones you hid instead. Did you look at her obituary picture? She was wearing one of the necklaces you stole. When Halftree told her they were modern jewels, she realized they must have been the ones you were suspected of stealing, and she knew that meant you were a jewel thief and a murderer. That's why she changed her will and left everything to the Historical Society."

"That's a lie!" Fairchild shouted. "She changed her will because those women at the Historical Society got to her and turned her against me. She would have never disowned me on her own. She loved me!" He thought about it. "Granted, she didn't know me very well. But, still . . ."

"You're right," Death said quickly. "She did love you. That's why she didn't go to the police. Why she hid the jewels again instead. But she also believed in justice. She wouldn't have completely gotten rid of evidence of a murder, even one committed by someone she loved. Wherever she put those jewels, she meant them to be found again after her death. *Think*, Fairchild! You played in this house when you were a kid. You knew about the secret compartment under the stairs and the secret entrance. What other hiding places are there? Somewhere an old lady could get to. Somewhere inside, most likely, because she hid them in the middle of winter."

"How do you know she hid them in the winter?"

"The picture in her obituary was taken at the Chamber of Commerce Christmas party. That must have been just after she found them. She'd have taken them to Halftree as soon as she could, and she wouldn't have worn them again once she knew what they really were."

Fairchild thought about it, eyes narrowed. "You've already been searching," he observed. "Where have you looked?"

"We've been looking in all the closets and cupboards and dresser drawers and things," Wren spoke up for the first time in a long time. "We looked in all the obvious places, but we haven't really checked for secret compartments or anything. There was a secret compartment in the desk in the library, but it just had a packet of old love letters in it. Look for drawers that aren't as deep as they should be. False books, maybe? A lot of people in old times had boxes made to look like Bibles or volumes of Shakespeare. There's a wall safe upstairs in a room furnished like an office, but it's standing open and there's nothing in it."

"Okay," Fairchild said. "Okay, those are good suggestions. I'll go look. You," he turned to Ten Oeck, "stay here and keep an eye on them."

Ten Oeck held his knife up, balancing it between his hands with one finger on the hilt and one on the tip. He spun it and grinned. "Yeah, I'll just stay here and keep an eye on them," he said.

Wren blanched. Death gave Ten Oeck a tight smile as Fairchild left the room.

"Good plan, there, genius. You stay here and play sadist with us while Fairchild goes off and finds the jewels himself. And I'm sure that, once he's got them, he'll be perfectly straightforward about coming back here and divvying them up with you."

Ten Oeck's face changed and he spun around and charged after Fairchild. "Hey! Wait just a minute! I'm coming with you!"

Death waited until their footfalls died away, then turned his attention to Wren, who was watching him with a fury growing in her eyes. Her gaze moved over his face and down to his torso. Taking stock of his injuries, he realized. If she'd had her atlatl to hand, Fairchild and Ten Oeck would both be shish kebabs.

"Are you okay?" she breathed.

He smiled for her benefit, felt the skin at the corner of his mouth pull against his cut lip. "I'm okay. Fairchild hits like a girl."

"I don't believe you."

"I'm a Marine. I'm fine. Are you okay? Have they hurt you?"

Her eyes filled with tears and Death saw red.

"Those sons-of-bitches cut off my braid, Death!"

He'd feared so much worse that he had to fight not to laugh with relief. "It's okay, sweetie. I've got it at the house. We can probably duct tape it back on or something."

While he talked, he was trying to slide the P38 out of its secret pocket on his waistband. He could just get the tips of his fingers under the leather, but he was having trouble getting hold of the tiny implement. If he dropped it, he knew, they were screwed.

Wren didn't answer for a long minute, only watching him with her tongue poking out the corner of her mouth. "Death?" she said at last, softly. "Don't be doing that if they come back in the room. It's pretty obvious that you're up to something."

"Yeah, I figured. We should have practiced this."

"So does that mean that, after we get out of here, I have an excuse to tie you up?"

215

"Probably be a good idea. And you should be able to do this too. We'll get you a couple of P38s and make you hiding places for them. And then I'll have an excuse to tie you up, too."

She smiled a watery smile at him. Putting on a brave face, he realized, and wondered which of them she was being brave for.

"Do you think there's a chance they'll find the jewels?"

"There's always a chance."

"And then what?" she asked, and he heard what she wasn't saying. *Will it be okay? Will they let us go? Are they going to kill us anyway?*

He knew she already knew the answer to that. She just wanted him to lie to her, to lie to them both, but he couldn't bring himself to do it.

"And then we'll cross that bridge when we come to it."

He had his fingertips on the P38 now and was edging it out of its pocket. Because of the angle his hands were tied, he couldn't get a good grip. He barely had hold of it between two fingers. Slowly, ever so slowly, he drew it loose. When it was free of the leather tag, he shifted and tucked it into his right hand, feeling the sharp corners dig into his palm. He turned it, bringing it up to put the edge of the hook against the zip tie around his wrists. The angle was awkward and he sawed at it desperately, unable to get much force behind each stroke. The situation reminded him of Tyrone Blount, trying to cut his way out of the cargo net with a pocket knife. Still, he refused to despair.

It was a can opener, dammit! A *Marine* can opener. It was designed to chew through metal. It would not be defeated by plastic.

There was a clatter of footsteps on the stairs out in the hallway and Death stopped trying to cut the plastic, straightened up and hid the P38 in his palm. Fairchild and Ten Oeck came back into the room, both looking sweaty and disheveled and angry.

216

"There's nothing here," Ten Oeck said. "We've looked every-where. There's nothing here." He shot Fairchild a look. "Can't I dissect one of them now?"

"In a minute," Fairchild said irritably. He was pacing the room, hand on his chin, thinking furiously. "You were wrong," he said to Death. "My aunt never found those jewels. She was just a batty old woman. You know what she wanted me to do, the last time she visited me in prison? She wanted me to write emails to a publishing company because some book had a white girl instead of a black girl on the cover. She was totally senile. She never found anything."

He stopped talking long enough to come over and stand in front of Death, stare him in the face. Death swallowed and tried not to look like he was up to something.

"I know who did, though," Fairchild exclaimed. "I've figured it out and I know exactly what happened."

"Okay … well … you want to enlighten us?"

"Certainly." Fairchild strode to the center of the room and turned with a flourish to face them. He reminded Death of the detective in an old, black-and-white whodunnit. *You're probably wondering why I called you all together*, Death thought. "It was …," he paused for effect, "the Historical Society!"

"The Historical Society?" Death asked in disbelief.

"The Historical Society?" Wren echoed.

"Obviously the Historical Society. It's the only thing that makes any sense."

"And your definition of 'sense' would be …?"

"They must have gotten her to let them in the house somehow. Asked for a tour or told her they were writing a treatise on blah-blah-blah architecture or something. Oh! Or slavery! She was a sucker for anything to do with slavery. Always going on about 'righting old wrongs' and so forth. Anyway, how isn't important. The important thing is, they got in the house, and while they were poking around in here, they found my jewels."

"But if the Historical Society stole the jewels," Death objected, "how did your aunt come to be wearing that necklace to the Christmas party?"

"They gave it to her. They probably showed her some of the jewels and let her think they were from the Civil War. They knew she'd have Josiah Halftree look at them and he'd tell her they weren't old enough. It was all a part of their dastardly plot to convince her that I was a thief and a murderer!"

Death decided to overlook the 'dastardly'. "You are a thief and a murderer."

Fairchild glared at him. "What does that have to do with anything?"

"Nothing. Sorry! Forget I mentioned it."

"Right, so they convinced her I was a thief and a murderer so that she'd write me out of her will and leave my house to them instead! And then, when she'd done it," he paused to give them each a brooding, baleful stare, "they killed her!"

For a long minute no one spoke. Then Death shook his head as if shaking water from his hair, or trying to rattle his brain into place. "I'm sorry? You think the Historical Society murdered Ava Fairchild?"

"They had to have. The timing is too coincidental otherwise."

Something prickled in the back of Death's mind, because there was something about timing that had been bothering him too. Something about the events surrounding Ava Fairchild's death.

Nothing that screamed 'murderous Historical Society', but something nonetheless.

"What do you mean by that? Explain to me, please?"

Fairchild shrugged. "She was wearing the necklace at Christmas. She re-wrote her will in January and in March, she died."

"She died in March," Death echoed.

"That's what I just said."

"She died in March!" A sudden rush of adrenaline ran through Death, a thrill of discovery and understanding so powerful that for a moment he forgot that he was sore and aching. That he was bound and that he and Wren were in imminent peril. He looked up and locked eyes with her.

"Remember I said before that something about the timing was bothering me?"

She nodded.

"That was it. Ava Fairchild died in March!" He grinned and looked around the room, from face to face. "I know where she hid the jewels."

TWENTY-ONE

"You figured out where the jewels are just because I reminded you that Aunt Ava died in March?" Declan Fairchild's voice dripped skepticism.

"Yes! I should have seen it before. I had all the information I needed, but I didn't put it together. Now I have."

"Okay, I'll bite. Tell me where they are. And if you're wrong…" He exchanged a meaningful glance with Ten Oeck. "Don't be wrong."

"In the pantry there's a shelf filled with jars of strawberry jam."

"Yeah, and?"

"The jewels are in the jam."

Fairchild snorted. "Now that's just stupid. Why would Aunt Ava have put my jewels in jars of strawberry jam? And even if she did, what would that have to do with her dying in March?"

"She was big on justice, you know that. Hell, she spent half her life trying to make up for the fact that her ancestors owned slaves. There was no way she was going to give you a pass on murder. But she'd already lost her husband and her daughter and she couldn't bear to see you go down too, so she hid the jewels where she thought they'd be found when she died. According to her will, those jars of jam were supposed to be donated to the food bank. The only reason they weren't was because you contested the will and by the time the court case was settled, everybody figured they were too old to eat."

"That doesn't mean anything. Aunt Ava always made jam and canned things. She liked to garden. And she always gave stuff away, a lot of it to the food bank."

"Right. Every year at Christmas, in fact. That's what you told me, right?" He looked at Wren and she nodded.

"Oh, my God! Death! That totally makes sense."

"In December, she gave away all the preserves and canned goods she'd made that year. When she died in March, her pantry should have still been empty."

"Big deal," Fairchild said. "So she made some more."

"But strawberries don't ripen until late May or June. She'd have to have bought them. And out-of-season fruit is expensive. She put the jewels in the strawberry jam."

Fairchild still looked skeptical. Ten Oeck looked bored and he was fiddling with his knife and staring longingly at Death.

"There's one way to find out," Wren said.

Fairchild hesitated, then motioned with his head to Ten Oeck and the two men stepped from the room. An argument broke out between them in low tones. Death couldn't hear every word, but he could hear enough to get the gist of it. He went back to work with his can opener, driven by a sense of urgency in the pit of his gut.

"Death?" Wren asked, "what are they doing?"

"Arguing." He wanted to spare her the fear that was lancing through him now, the knowledge that they might be almost out of time.

"Sweetheart," she said, very gently, "I'm not a child. They're arguing about what to do with us, aren't they?"

The zip tie was beginning to give. He would soon be free, but that wasn't enough. He'd have to get Wren free, too, and he could feel time slipping away from them. It pained him to admit it, but he'd learned from bitter experience that he was no longer physically able to take out one man, let alone two of them, and both armed. He needed a plan, and a distraction, and he needed help.

"Fairchild told Ten Oeck that, whether or not the jewels are there, we're no further use to him. He wants him to come back in and—" he broke off, couldn't finish.

"Kill us?"

"Yeah." Death swallowed. "But, for once, Ten Oeck is thinking with his brain instead of his knife hand. Fairchild thinks I'm right about the jewels. Ten Oeck knows that, and he knows that Fairchild is trying to distract him so he can take the loot and run. Or, more likely, get the drop on him and shoot him in the back."

"What are we going to do?"

"I don't know. We'll think of something."

The argument outside the door ended and Death could hear two sets of footfalls going down the hall to the pantry. He sawed harder, gaining a little more movement with each passing second as he looked frantically around the parlor, seeking something he could use as a weapon. There was nothing. He could probably bar the door, but it wouldn't hold for more than a few seconds. Even if it was long enough to get Wren free from the chair, and she was much more securely fastened than he, all Fairchild had to do was go outside and shoot them through the window. He considered that briefly, as a less-painful alternative to dying at Ten Oeck's hands, but if he understood Fairchild, he suspected the bastard wouldn't shoot to kill.

Death's zip tie fell away as he heard Fairchild and Ten Oeck returning. He caught it and closed it in his fist so it wouldn't fall on the floor and betray that he was free. Then he stood back up, trying to stretch his cramping arm muscles without being obvious about it.

Calculating odds and not liking the answers he was getting.

Their captors came into the room, each carrying three jars of strawberry jam. Fairchild leered at Wren.

"I figured we might as well bring it in here. Even if there aren't any jewels, jam can be used for lots of things."

He set two of the jars he was carrying down on a side table, tucked the third under his left arm and used his right hand to twist at the cap. It took a few seconds, but then it broke loose and turned with a coarse rasp. He unscrewed it. It was just a ring around the outside. When it was free and he had set it aside, the jar was still covered by a brass-colored lid. The thin orange line of a rubber seal separated the metal from the glass jar. Fairchild tried prising it up with his fingernails, turning the jar this way and that so that it caught the late sun coming in the window, making the jam shine with a ruby light, like fresh blood.

He gave up, sighed and glanced briefly at Ten Oeck and his butcher knife before digging a small penknife out of his own pocket to break the seal with.

They don't trust each other, Death thought. *Okay, they never did. But the closer they are to finding the jewels, the less trust there is.* He wondered how he could use that against them.

The lid separated with a soft *pop*. Fairchild glanced around, shrugged, and tipped the jam up. It stayed stubbornly in the jar. He sighed and set it down again. "Don't anybody go anywhere."

He left the room quickly, rapid footfalls charting his progress down the hall and back. In just a few seconds he had returned with a rubber spatula. He slipped it into the jam, just skimming the top of the confection, scooped a little out and, with a leer, spread it across Wren's bared chest, just above the top of her bra.

She leaned away from him, looking ill, and Death schooled his temper. There would be time for payback later.

"Is there anything in there or not?" Ten Oeck demanded.

"Sure. Jam." Fairchild dug the spatula into the jar, scooped out a great blob and let it fall to the floor. He stuck the spatula back in and it came up with a great wad of jam-covered plastic. "Well, I'll be damned."

Setting the jar down, he brushed the jam away, absently licking it off his fingers, and revealed a zip-lock bag. He opened the bag and poured the contents out into his palm. A pile of gemstones shone in the muted sunlight. A square of white paper fluttered out beside them. Fairchild dropped the bag, closed his fist around the jewels and pulled the paper out to read it.

"These jewels are evidence in a murder investigation," he read. "There is a reward for finding them. Take them to the police and tell them they came from the Fairchild house. Ava Fairchild."

Fairchild looked up, shock and disbelief reflected in his face. "That *bitch*!" he exploded. "She was going to send me away for murder! God, I wish she was still alive so I could kill her!" He shredded the paper and went to drop the jewels in his pocket.

"Hey! Wait a minute! Half of those are mine. We had a deal!" Ten Oeck was in his face, hand outstretched, clutching his butcher knife menacingly.

Death weighed his chances of jumping them now, causing Ten Oeck to stab Fairchild and getting the gun before Ten Oeck stabbed him.

Too much of a long shot, he decided. And they were standing too close to Wren.

"I'm not taking them," Fairchild said. "I'm just putting them in my pocket until we get them all out of the jars. Then we can take them out and divvy them up."

"Yeah," Death cut in. "You can trust your old buddy Declan, Ten Oeck. Not like he's gonna put thirty jewels in his pocket and only bring out twenty when it's time to share them out. He wouldn't do a thing like that."

"You shut up!" Fairchild bellowed.

"I'm not stupid," Ten Oeck said. "You don't put them in your pocket. They stay out where we both can see them."

"I can't hold them and open all the other jars too!"

"Then I'll hold them."

"I'm not gonna let you hold them."

They glared at each other and Death hoped they'd come to blows. If it got down to one-on-one, with the element of surprise on his side, he'd take the chance.

Fairchild backed down. "Okay, fine. Go out to the kitchen and find something to put them in."

"You go out to the kitchen. I'm not leaving you here alone with them."

They both looked around the room and their eyes settled on Wren.

"We'll have the girl hold them," Fairchild decided. "She's not going anywhere and she couldn't hide them anyplace we couldn't find them."

"She could drop them down her shirt," Ten Oeck objected.

"Like I said, she couldn't hide them anyplace we couldn't find them. Okay?"

"Okay."

They descended on Wren and Death held his breath as Ten Oeck used the big butcher knife to slice the zip ties holding her arms down.

"Cup your hands," Fairchild told her.

She did and he dumped the jewels into them. He walked around behind her and whispered in her ear. Death couldn't hear what he was saying, but he could see his face so he could read his lips.

"Don't drop them. If you drop one, I'll cut off one of your boyfriend's fingers."

Wren blanched and nodded and held the gems tight in trembling hands. Fairchild and Ten Oeck turned to opening the rest of the jars and Death watched and waited and bided his time.

———

Jar after jar yielded up treasure and the pile in Wren's hands grew and grew. She fought the shaking wracking her body and concentrated on holding them. She didn't doubt for a minute that Fairchild had meant his threat, and the consequences of dropping anything were unthinkable.

When they found the necklace Ava had worn in her obituary photo they fastened it mockingly around Wren's neck. They slid rings onto her fingers and pulled out her own cheap earrings to replace them with priceless gems. She had never been so surrounded by so many pretty things, and she had never been more miserable. She wondered, if they survived this, if she'd ever be able to look at another piece of jewelry.

"That's all of them."

The floor was a slippery mess of strawberry jam. Fairchild and Ten Oeck had scraped out all the jars, then spread the jam thin across the floor to be sure they hadn't missed any jewels. Wren's hands were full to overflowing.

"Do we divide them up now?" Ten Oeck asked.

Fairchild shook his head. "First, let's find something to put them in." He looked around the room, crossed to a corner curio cabinet and came back with a large crystal vase. He knelt in front of Wren and helped her pour the shimmering, multicolored pile into it. "Don't drop any," he reminded her playfully and she shivered with the laughter in his voice and the cold light in his eyes.

Ten Oeck leaned over his shoulder, watching like a hawk and reaching in to help from time to time. They pulled the rings from her fingers, dropping them in the vase one by one, but when Ten Oeck reached for the necklace and earrings Fairchild stopped him.

"Let's leave those where they are," he said. "Just for now. I think it's time we stop for a little celebration."

"*Now* do I get to kill somebody?" Ten Oeck demanded.

"Patience. Patience." Fairchild stood up, carefully circled the mess on the floor and went to stand in front of Death. "You know, we would never have found these if it weren't for Mr. Bogart here. I think we should give him some kind of reward."

"You're not giving him any of my jewels," Ten Oeck warned.

"No, no. I wasn't thinking that kind of reward."

"You could let us go," Death suggested.

Fairchild made a show of considering it, then shook his head. "No, that's not what I was thinking either. Actually, what I had in mind was," he gave Wren a heated, lusty stare, "I'm going to let you watch me play with your girlfriend." He turned and addressed Ten Oeck. "*Then* you can kill him. As slowly as you like."

"No! Wait! Stop! Don't hurt her!"

Fairchild, approaching Wren purposefully, ignored Death's pleas. He went around behind Wren's chair and leaned down. She could feel his breath against the nape of her neck and then he was nuzzling her throat, tugging at the priceless necklace with his teeth and licking her skin. His arms circled the chair, hands roaming over her stomach, slipping under her blouse and caressing her breasts. His voice in her ear was low and throaty.

"I'm going to enjoy this a lot more when we're both naked and there's no chair between us."

"Fairchild, listen!" Death's voice was desperate. "I want to make a deal!"

"A deal?" Fairchild's hands stilled and he snorted against her neck in disbelief. "What do you imagine you have to bargain with?"

"You can't hurt her," Death said. "Do anything you want to me, but you can't hurt her."

Fairchild looked at Wren, sitting rigid with tears on her cheeks. "He keeps saying that. I suppose you think it's endearing, but honestly, he's just getting on my nerves."

"If she cooperates with you, will you let her go afterward?"

"Cooperates how?" Fairchild asked, voice thoughtful.

"Cooperates," Death repeated. "Participates. Is willing."

Wren stared at Death, horrified by the suggestion, but he was locked in a staring contest with Fairchild and didn't look at her.

"Why should I care if she's willing or not? I have a gun and Ten Oeck has a knife and I'm stronger than she is. I can do anything to her I want."

"You can do anything to *her*," Death said. "But if she cooperates, she can do things to *you.*"

Fairchild thought about it. "Yeah?"

"Yeah." Death looked the other man in the eye. "I'm telling you, my girl has talent. She can make you feel things you never even *dreamed* about."

There was a short silence and then Fairchild looked at her. "She can show me what she's got and I'll think about it," he conceded. "That's the best you're going to get."

He walked away long enough to set his gun on a side table, then came back to her. He pulled out his pocket knife and cut the rope around her waist and the zip ties holding her ankles to the chair. He pulled her up, slid one hand inside her blouse and bent to continue sucking at her neck.

She looked over at Death again and this time he met her eyes, giving her an intense stare.

"I'm sorry, baby," he said, "but you know how it is. He's got the dick. He calls the shots."

She felt her eyes widen in sudden understanding and suddenly all the fear and apprehension melted away, dissolved on a rising, boiling lava pool of rage. Fury ran through her like white-hot plasma and she channeled it into action.

Fairchild tipped back his head and sighed in anticipation as she unzipped his fly and reached for his family jewels.

———

When Fairchild started groping Wren, Ten Oeck turned his back to them and came over to stand close to Death. Death ignored him, trying desperately to bargain with Fairchild. He hated the look on

Wren's face, hated every second that the bastard was touching her. His hands were free and he wanted more than anything to storm across the room and take Fairchild down, but he knew if he tried it his body would betray him.

Just the rage he felt was weakening him, messing with his breathing, making him light-headed.

"He has the dick, he calls the shots," he told Wren, and saw in her eyes the instant she understood. He couldn't take them out alone. He needed her help.

Ten Oeck was feeling Death's bicep. He ran his hand over the Marine's stomach, then up across his chest. He pulled out the neckline of Death's tee shirt and looked down it.

"You have marvelous musculature," he breathed. He sounded turned on and Death *so* did not want to go there. "Abs, delts, pecs, glutes." He squeezed Death's ass and ran a hand down the inside of his thigh. "God, you're like a smorgasbord. I don't even know where to start."

He was in front of Death now, blocking his sight, but Death heard the sound of a zipper and Fairchild's sighed, "oh, baby!" Then the screaming started.

He had expected Ten Oeck to go to his cohort's aid, but instead the other man just pointed and laughed. It wasn't the distraction he was planning on, but it was distraction enough.

Death reached back and closed his fingers around the loose riser that covered the secret compartment under the stair. He swung it around in an arc and smashed it into Ten Oeck's head. It was a glancing blow and didn't completely disable him, but it stunned him and it knocked him into the middle of the oil-slick of strawberry jam. Careful to avoid the jam himself, Death ran for the door into the hall. Fairchild's screaming had subsided into a high-pitched, desperate squeal, but he could hear Ten Oeck stumbling along and cursing behind him.

He was halfway across the hall when he felt Ten Oeck's hand on his arm, dragging at him. Just the effort of swinging the stair riser and the short run had him seeing spots. He didn't have stamina to spare for a real fight. He spun, lashing out with his right hand. He was still holding onto the P38 and the sharp edge gouged into Ten Oeck's arm, drawing blood.

Ten Oeck released him and stared down in disbelief.

"You hurt me! You absolute bastard! You hurt me!"

By the time he'd finished shouting, Death was at the door to the morning room. He crossed to the window seat with Ten Oeck closing the distance between them rapidly. He flipped up the seat, pulled out his gun and turned to draw a bead on the other man.

"Stop or I'll shoot! I mean it! Stop now!"

Ten Oeck blind with rage just rushed at him. He was holding his butcher knife underhand, with his thumb closest to the blade, and away from his body. It was a position used by someone who knew what they were doing in a knife fight and Death knew he'd be deadly if he got close enough to strike.

He centered the gun on Ten Oeck's chest, took a steadying breath and squeezed the trigger on the exhale. He felt the jolt of the recoil run up along his arm at the same time Ten Oeck's heart pumped out a stream of blood that shot across the room and covered him in gore.

With a deep sigh born of a mixture of relief and regret, he lowered the gun and looked up as Wren's footsteps crossed the hall and she appeared in the doorway.

Her clothes were askew, her suddenly short hair wild around her head, her face red and her eyes glittering. She held her arms carefully to the side, like a surgeon who has scrubbed and doesn't want to contaminate herself.

"Are you okay?" she saw the blood. "Oh, God!"

"It's all right, baby. It isn't mine."

She crossed the room, stepped around the body and came over to lean against him—a hug without hands.

"Where's Fairchild?"

"Still in the Naked Dead Guy room. I think he says he wants his mommy. He sounds like he's been breathing helium, so it's kind of hard to tell." She looked down at Ten Oeck. "We need to call 911."

Death picked up his cell. "I got that."

"Good. I want to go wash my hands. With bleach." She started for the doorway, then stopped, turned back and read his face. "You didn't have any choice, Death."

"Yeah, I know. And it's not like I've never killed a man before. But I don't like it. I've never liked it."

"That's the difference between you and him."

"Yeah, I guess." He gave her a sad smile. "One more ghost for the Campbell house."

TWENTY-TWO

"WHEN YOU SAID THIS auction would be huge, you weren't kidding!"

Wren glanced around the crowded house and grounds of the Campbell house, trying to see it all through Death's eyes. Heaven knew, it was better than seeing it through her own. She still had nightmares about the things that had happened here.

Today the future museum was a madhouse. The auction had drawn in a huge crowd, with serious art and antique dealers and collectors and regular auction-goers supplemented by curiosity seekers. There were cars parked in the surrounding blocks with plates from as far away as Michigan, and Cameron had pointed out a photographer from the Associated Press.

Death, arguably a story in his own right, had been keeping a low profile.

The first thing he'd done, when he'd gotten the reward money for finding the stolen jewels, was buy Wren a big bouquet of roses from a pricey florist. She'd accepted them with false enthusiasm and poorly-concealed disappointment, and he'd laughed at her when she admitted that she preferred the flowers he picked for her himself.

For the most part, though, he remained as frugal as he'd always been. He'd paid taxes on the reward, paid up his professional and vehicle insurance for a year, and signed a one-year lease on a combination office/studio apartment above an old department store in downtown East Bledsoe Ferry, and he still had just over $80,000 in the bank.

At the moment all the action was outside. Roy's loudspeaker-amplified voice followed them across the porch and into the hall.

"And-a-seventy-and-a five-and-a eighty-and-a-five-do-I-gotta-five-and-a-one-that's-a-eighty-one-and-a-two-and-a ..."

Wren dragged her feet on the threshold, still reluctant to enter, even though she'd been here a hundred times since That Day. The house was empty—walking in the entryway was like being trapped inside a drum. The sale items were spread out on the lawn and in the back garden and the things the historical society meant to keep had been locked in the attics for their protection. Only some of the artwork remained, carefully hung around the walls, behind a podium one of the grandsons had dug up in an outbuilding. Grigsby, hired off-duty to work security for the auction, kept a watchful eye on two or three dozen well-dressed people who milled around studying the pieces on display.

Death paused to watch them. "I'm still surprised you're selling the artwork."

"They're keeping some," Wren said, "but the insurance alone would be outrageous if they kept it all."

"Yeah, I understand that. What surprises me is that *you're* selling it. I thought you had to send artwork to some big, fancy auction house in New York or London or someplace."

Wren shrugged. "Merchandise is merchandise. We're doing the art as a separate auction within an auction. And Doris is an expert appraiser. She's advertised in all the right places. Actually, we might do better than a big city auction house. It's not the auctioneer who sets the price, you know. It's the bidders. And we're apt to draw a lot of optimistic art enthusiasts who think they're going to come out in the sticks and make a steal."

"Okay, but as I understood, some of this is pretty high-dollar stuff. Are you really set up to handle selling things for that much money?"

"Death!" She sighed, exasperated. "We do vehicle and heavy equipment auctions. We sell *real estate*. Last Wednesday we sold a two-hundred-acre dairy farm for a quarter of a million dollars."

"Well, I guess that answers that," he said, and went on into the office.

The massive desk where Wren had found Obadiah's love letters was the only piece of furniture still in the house, and Leona and Doris were set up there, where they could use the wall safe to protect the larger-than-average proceeds. At the moment, they were busy signing up a few stragglers and assigning them bid numbers.

"Better give me a number, too," Death said. "I could still use stuff for my office and apartment."

Doris and Leona exchanged a glance.

"What do you think, Doris? Do we want to give this boy a number?"

"Well, now, I don't know. Does he have any identification on him? We wouldn't want to give him a number and then find out he's an imposter or anything."

Death grinned at their teasing and fished out his driver's license.

Doris handed Death a roughly square piece of poster board with his number on it.

"Six-seventy-two?" Wren was shocked. "Really? There's almost seven hundred people here?"

"What can we say?" Leona shrugged. "Antiques and bloodstains make for a powerful draw." She smiled at Death. "Honestly, unless there's something specific you're interested in, you'd be better off waiting for a less spectacular auction to get any furniture you need. Was there anything in particular that caught your fancy?"

He shrugged. "I thought, since they're selling them, maybe I could pick up one of old Obadiah's political cartoons, just for a souvenir, you know?"

Doris shook her head. "Oh, I wouldn't get your hopes up there, honey. We're selling the four of them as a lot and there's a collector here from Chicago. Marlon Obermeier? Wealthy political junkie. Very deep pockets and a bit of a fanatic."

"Oh, well," Death was philosophical. "Just my luck."

"Here," she offered him a small booklet. "There's a special catalog for the artwork. Take a look at it. Maybe you'll see something else that strikes your fancy."

Death took the booklet, folded it and tucked it into his shirt pocket along with his number. Still more people were pouring into the room, some of them seeking numbers and some of them leaving early with their purchases. Death and Wren slipped out and went to explore the rest of the auction. As they went through the entry hall, they passed a group of middle-aged women standing in the parlor doorway and peering into the room.

"I think this is where they found the naked dead guy," one of them was saying.

Wren groaned and slapped her own forehead with her palm and Death laughed, put an arm around her shoulder and led her outside.

In order to get through the auction in one day, Sam and Roy were working on opposite sides of the old house, both calling at once. Death and Wren spent the morning going back and forth between them, helping set up merchandise, keeping track of bids and, in one instance, breaking up a screaming, hair-pulling match over who outbid whom for an antique butter churn. Wren took turns at the microphones, spelling each of the brothers, and Death had a quiet word with a would-be shoplifter, who subsequently emptied her pockets and slunk away.

They got lunch from the food cart that was set up at the curb, filling the air with the scent of barbecue, and ate it sitting in a quiet corner of the garden and watching the chaos from a distance. When they ventured back inside, Sam had moved indoors and the art auction was under way.

Doris came over to stand beside them. "They're selling the Healey political cartoons now," she told them. "It's up to twenty-five thousand. That's Mr. Obermeier there," she pointed out a tall, thin man in his sixties. "I expect he'll get a deal on them. As a collection they're worth at least forty thousand, but he'll be willing to go well over that and all the serious collectors here know it, so I doubt anyone will bother to bid him up that high."

"That much?" Death fished the art catalog out of his pocket and opened it, finding his place as the bidding climbed toward thirty thousand dollars. Wren grinned to herself as she heard him whisper softly, "holy crap!"

"And I have thirty-one thousand, five hundred," Sam said. This type of auction called for a less boisterous salesman, and he had slowed his speech to normal speeds. He turned his attention back to the woman who'd been bidding against Obermeier and Wren saw in her eyes when she decided to back down. She shook her head and Sam looked around the room. "Anyone else? That's thirty-one, five, going once! Going twice! And—"

"FIFTY THOUSAND!"

It seemed everyone in the room jumped, Wren especially, at the deep, powerful voice that broke out beside her. In truth, Death looked a little startled himself, but he caught Sam's eye and repeated his words. "I bid fifty thousand dollars."

"Death!" Wren squeaked. "Are you *insane*?"

"Trust me," he said. "I'll explain later. Right now, just trust me."

Obermeier looked like he'd bitten a lemon. "If this is some kind of attempt by the auction house to bid the price up, you're going to regret it."

Death looked him in the eye. "What I'm trying to do is outbid you. If you think it's a trick then teach me a lesson. Drop out."

Obermeier considered it for a long moment, then turned back to the podium.

"Fifty-five thousand."

"Fifty-six," Death countered.

"Fifty-six, five."

"Fifty-seven."

"Fifty-eight."

"Sixty." Death spoke with no hesitation.

Wren grabbed hold of the banister for support. The room was suddenly stifling, with a dearth of air and an electricity running through the crowd that made the hair stand up on her arms.

Obermeier studied Death for a long minute, eyes narrowed.

"Sixty-five."

"Sixty-five thousand," Sam repeated. He looked helplessly at Death.

Doris tugged at Death's sleeve. "Honey, those pictures aren't worth that much!"

"Sixty-eight," Death bid.

"Seventy," Obermeier said. There was an air of finality about it. Wren couldn't say what it was, but instinct developed over the years of watching people bid at auctions told her the man was nearing his limit. Plain old arithmetic and a knowledge of Death's finances told her that he was nearing his.

Wren didn't know what to hope for. Obviously Death had his heart set on getting those pictures, but if he did, he was going to be broke again. There was just no way she could see this ending well.

"Seventy-one," Death said.

"Seventy-one, five," Obermeier countered.

"Seventy-two."

Obermeier stood up straighter, put his hands in his pockets and turned to look Death straight in the eye. "Seventy-five thousand dollars."

Death turned to Wren. "Do you trust me?" he asked, and what could she say.

"I trust you with my life," she told him. "How could I possibly not trust you with your own money?"

He grinned and turned back to face Sam. "Seventy-six thousand dollars," he said.

"You're insane." The collector finally shook his head. "I'm out. If he wants them that badly, he can have them."

Death slumped in relief and drew in a deep breath.

Sam paused, gavel raised, and gave Death a grave, concerned look.

"Son, are you sure about this? Because, when I bring this gavel down, the sale will be final."

Death met his eye. "I'm sure."

Sam shrugged. "All right, then. That's a collection of four political cartoons by the artist Obadiah Healey and it's SOLD to number 672."

———

It took Death most of the rest of the afternoon to go to his bank and argue them into giving him a certified check for most of the money he had left in his account. By the time he got back to the Campbell house the auction was winding down and the last stragglers were packing up their loot and making their escape.

The four cartoons were still hanging in their place on the wall. Death lifted them down, one by one, grinning like a maniac, and carried them into the office to pay for them. Wren was there, waiting for him, with the Keystone twins and their wives. He set the paintings down on the desk and pulled his number from his pocket.

"Six seventy two?" he asked.

"Well, let's see." Leona made a show of looking in her log books and digging out the file card with his information on it. "I have one purchase, four pictures, for seventy-six thousand dollars."

"Will you take a check?" He offered her the certified check and she took it and gave him a receipt.

"Okay," Roy said. "Now, are you going to explain yourself, or is this some kind of psychotic break with reality?"

Death laughed. "I would be glad to explain myself. Would it be alright if we close the door and lock it first?"

Sam went to close and lock the door and Death pulled the auction catalog from his pocket.

"So, who was it who put together this catalog, anyway?"

"Me," Doris said.

"Doris," Wren supplied. "She's our art expert, remember?"

"Ah ha. I see. And you didn't bother to read it before the sale at all?"

"Well, I've been busy. And we all knew what the stuff for sale was."

"Did you? Really? Are you *sure*?"

Sam and Roy were standing side by side, arms crossed, and for once it was obvious that they were identical twins in spite of their different clothes.

"If he doesn't start talking soon, I say one of us should kick him," Roy said.

"I'll flip you for it."

"Wren," Death said, "remember when you found those letters and we were reading them?"

"Before or after you started ripping each other's clothes off?" Leona asked.

Death felt his cheeks flame, but plowed ahead. "Before," he said. "In the first part of the letter he said that Mr. Monroe liked Gentlemen Dancing, remember?"

Wren nodded.

Death held up the top picture, the one of smiling men shaking hands and hiding knives behind their backs. "This is Gentlemen Dancing. All of these cartoons have names."

"That's not unusual," Doris said. "Please tell me you didn't just buy these because they have names?"

"It's because of what their names are," he said. When he spoke again it was in a high-pitched, feminine voice. "Oh, you poor thing! Those bad men took all your pretty jewels!"

He paused to look around at his audience and Wren, catching on first, gasped and sank down on the edge of the desk. He switched to a second voice, still feminine but lower pitched, with a deep Southern accent.

"They didn't get them. Ah hid 'em good."

"God in Heaven," Leona said. "Millie Weeks is gonna go postal."

"Tell me where," Death continued in the first woman's voice. "I'll get them for you." He grinned and went back to the second voice. "Look behind The Seventh Stone," he said, lifting the picture that showed Maryland as a stone in the nation's foundation. "Stars in the Water," he switched to the cartoon about the War of 1812, with the tattered reflection of Old Glory, "and See All The Pretty Colors," he finished, brandishing the last cartoon with the frontiersmen at the tailor shop.

"You think the pictures are a clue to where the jewels are?" Roy asked.

"I think the jewels are in the pictures," Death said. He turned Gentlemen Dancing over and showed them the back. The back of the frame was open, with the back of the matting clearly visible. Then he turned the others over, one by one. The backs of the frames were covered with heavy, yellowing paper tacked on with rusted brads. Death picked up Stars in the Water and shook it gently and it made a noise like sand and gravel moving through a gold miner's sluice.

"And you figured this out when?" Sam asked dryly.

"Just as you were about to sell them to Obermeier for thirty-one, five." Death took out his pocket knife and slit the paper on the back of Stars in the Water on three sides. He peeled it back and the cavity it had closed off was completely filled with a tangle of tarnished jewelry. He repeated the process with the other two pictures and the six of them stood there staring in silent awe at the long-lost muddle of rare metals and precious gems.

"I can't believe we're the first people to see these since the Civil War." Doris said.

"So what do you think now?" Death asked her. "Did I get my money's worth?"

"Yes, and then some, I should say. Leona's right, Millie's going to have kittens. She has no call to complain, though. She's the one who proofread the catalog. She should have figured it out herself."

"What are you going to do with it?" Sam asked.

Death shrugged. "I haven't really thought that far ahead. Sell most of it, probably. Donate some to the museum, maybe. I got a safe deposit box, but the bank's closed now so I'll probably take it to the police station and ask the chief to lock it up overnight."

"You could cover your girlfriend in diamonds and jewels," Roy suggested.

"No !" Wren and Death said simultaneously.

Death picked gingerly through the tangled mess of jewelry, grinned suddenly, and worked an elaborate serpentine necklace free.

"I've got an idea! We could play dress-up."

Wren looked at him askance. "You want to play dress-up?"

"Well, *I* don't want to dress up. I just thought it would be fun for you to dress up. See, I remember seeing this necklace in an old picture, and I was thinking you could wear what the lady in the picture was wearing and imitate the pose and everything. Art come to life, sort of."

"That's a clever idea," Leona said. "And you could take pictures and display them side by side."

"We could do that," Death agreed. He was biting the inside of his cheek.

"I don't know where I'd get a hoop skirt," Wren said. "I suppose I could make one..."

"Oh, you don't need to worry about that. The lady in the picture wasn't wearing a hoop skirt. I think it was probably from before they were popular."

"Not Carolina then? What picture was it? Do you know who she was?"

"Well, I assume it was Eustacia Healey."

"Eustacia Healey? Where did you see a picture of ... *oh!*"

"Yeah, that picture."

"The one in the, um ..."

"The one in the love letters. Remember? The classy porn?"

"She was wearing this necklace?"

"And nothing else." Death leaned forward and clasped the necklace around Wren's neck, then laughed at her as she stammered and stuttered. Her face turned as red as her hair.

But she didn't say no.

EPILOGUE

"DEATH?" WREN SAID. "I think it's done now."

He slid out from under his Jeep, parked in her driveway. Wren sat on the porch steps, Lucy at her feet and Thomas watching from the newel post with a bored expression as she fought with the crank of an old-fashioned wooden ice cream freezer.

He wiped his hands carefully on an old rag, went over and easily spun the handle a couple of times.

"It's not frozen yet?" she despaired. "Remind me again why I got this thing instead of a nice electric one that does the turning for you?"

"You thought it was quaint," he grinned.

"Quaint, right." She groaned. "Listen, next time I think something silly like that you—" She broke off and he turned to follow her gaze. A strange car had pulled up to the curb in front of the house.

While they watched, a man got out of the car. Death registered his uniform first and, even after ten months, pain stabbed through him like a knife to the heart.

Wren must have read something in his body language. She turned to him with worry in her blue eyes.

"It's okay." He released the crank from the freezer lid, lifted the lid and took the ice cream out of the slushy mixture of half-melted ice and rock salt inside. "I was only teasing you. This is done. You can put it in the freezer and it'll be just fine."

"But that man …?"

"I know. I need to talk to him. You go on. We'll be in in a minute."

Wren took the ice cream and went inside and Death stood and walked down to meet the stranger, who had been watching them from the sidewalk. He was a thin, middle-aged black man and he stood almost at attention, holding a briefcase. He offered Death his hand.

"Sergeant Bogart? I'm Captain Jonathan Cairn, of the St. Louis Fire Department."

"Cap. I know." Death took his hand in a firm grip. "Randy told me a lot about you."

"And he told us a lot about you. I'd wanted to meet with you earlier," the captain said. "I know how close the two of you were. This must all have been incredibly hard on you. I haven't had any way to get hold of you, though."

"Yeah, things have been pretty messed up. I actually thought about looking you up a couple of times, but I didn't know what I'd say. Would you like to come in?"

They went in the house and settled in the living room. Wren was in the kitchen, pretending she hadn't been peeking out the front window, and she came out to say hello.

"Honey, this is Captain Cairn. He was my brother's commanding officer. Captain—"

"Call me Cap. Everyone does."

Death shot him a faint grin. "Cap, this is my girlfriend, Wren Morgan."

"Miss Morgan, a pleasure to meet you."

"And you. Would you like some coffee?"

"Yes, please."

They settled around the coffee table and Cap set his briefcase on the table and opened it. "One reason I needed to see you is because we still have to settle your brother's estate."

Death was surprised. "It's not already settled?"

"No. You didn't know?"

"By the time I woke up in Germany, it seemed like everything was already done. I just figured my ex-wife got any money and spent it while I was overseas."

"I see." Cap rustled some papers. "Actually there was a complication. The day before Bogie—Randy—"

"It's okay," Death said with a wry grin. "I was Bogie in the Marine Corps, too."

"Right." Cap spared him a brief smile. "The day before Bogie died he got word that you'd been killed in action. Glad that turned out not to be true, by the way."

"Thanks," Death nodded.

"Anyway, that morning he got a call from, ah, your ex-wife?"

"Madeline."

"Madeline. Right. They had a bit of an altercation and the upshot was that he re-wrote his will at the last minute. He left everything to the fire station—I don't think he could think of anyone else right then and he was determined that, if anything happened to him, Madeline wasn't going to profit by it. After he died and you were found alive, Madeline filed to contest the will, arguing that he wouldn't have written you out of it if he knew you were still alive. Frankly, we agree, and there shouldn't be any problem with having that will thrown out and his previous will reinstated. However, we can't just do it on our own."

Death sighed and looked down at the floor between his feet.

Cap's voice softened. "Are you alright talking about this, son?"

"Yeah, I guess. It just … feels kinda like blood money, you know?"

"I know, but your brother would have wanted you to have it. I tried contacting you through Madeline, but after you divorced I wasn't able to get in touch with her. I just happened to see your name in the news and the police chief here knew where to find you. Anyway, I've got some papers here for you, so we can finally get this taken care of. Also," He reached into his briefcase. "I thought that maybe you'd like to have this."

He pulled out a silver shield, set against red velvet in a burnished silver frame. He offered it to Death, who took it with a puzzled frown.

"It's your brother's badge," Cap said.

"Yeah, I know but … did he have two? Because I already have one the coroner sent me."

He got up and went to a curio cabinet. Though he slept at his own apartment, Wren's place was quickly becoming home. His pictures and his few mementos sat on the shelves and hung on the walls beside hers now. He came back with a small box containing a copy of the badge in Cap's hand.

Cap took it with a frown. "Did the coroner say where he got this?"

"He said he took it off the body."

"That's impossible. The morning he died, Bogie snapped the back off his badge. We got called out before he had time to fix it. When he went into that fire, his shield was lying on my desk."

THE END

© About Faces Photography

ABOUT THE AUTHOR

Loretta Ross is a writer and historian who lives and works in rural Missouri. She is an alumna of Cottey College and holds a BA in archaeology from the University of Missouri–Columbia. She has loved mysteries since she first learned to read. *Death and the Redheaded Woman* is her first published novel.